The Purest of Pain

Anna Dennis

Apex Publishing

Anna Dennis

The Purest of Pain

ISBN: 0-9706257-1-5

Printed in the United States of America

10 9 8 7 6 5 4 3 2 1

For all my literary sisters and brothers in the struggle, always pursue your passion...this road will lead you to your dreams.

Anna Dennis

I Thankfully Acknowledge...

GOD, for through Him all things are possible
and nothing impossible.

My husband, Edward, my best friend...
my everything, words simply escape me.

Ariana, my Angel here on earth.

My mother, Merceal Swezey, for your undying love and support.

All my family, friends, peers and book buyers
who first gave me an audience.

Bernard Henderson of Alexander Book Company
for singing my praises.

Debra Roland, my BBWG partner for sharing your vision with me.

Fran Wessel, my editor for helping me refine my craft.

Dario Sanchez of V.C. Design
for bringing Devin, Taylor and Ted to life...beautifully.

The Purest of Pain

*And with the stroke of a pen
and the passion of our words,
we can influence the world...*

*~Life is not measured by the number of breaths we take,
but by the moments that take our breath away~*

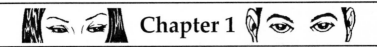 **Chapter 1**

Bright sunlight seeped through the wooden shutters and seared golden rays across Taylor's brown face. She squinted, placing a pillow over her face as she turned her back to the window. For most people Mondays were the worst, but for her, it was definitely Friday. She was already counting down the hours though her day hadn't even begun.

It wasn't that she didn't like her job, in fact, quite the contrary, she loved it. As Vice President of Human Resources for a large technology company, she found her role more like that of a therapist-listening to peoples problems day in and day out. The only difference was unlike a therapist; she actually had to solve problems instead of sending her clients a bill and asking them to come back in a week. Because of her excellent rapport with most of the executives in the organization, solving problems was the easy part. Sure there were a few who would never get past the fact that an African-American woman was in charge of Human Resources. What they didn't know was that HR was the only department that did allow a certain amount of growth for many minorities and more specifically, women.

Devin Harris, Taylor's husband, had been the exception.

Devin escaped the very real likelihood of becoming a janitor, or working in the mailroom. The disdain of being an "Uncle Tom" was the driving force behind his starting his own DotCom. Although for now, he did not have to deal with the bureaucracy and politics that went on in a corporation. When faced with it, he was intelligent enough to play ball with the big boys. Devin was co-owner of a dot com start-up that he and an old college friend, Ted, had started almost a year ago. They had hoped their company, which would offer not only free internet service but also the ability to download the latest music CD's, would be the first of its kind. However, several other companies with the same idea had beaten them to the punch by going public on the US stock exchange. This had forced them to make many modifications to their web site, product and services as well as address certain copyright issues.

Taylor grudgingly threw the covers back and swung her long, shapely legs over the elegant, four-poster, cherry wood bed. She pressed the lever on the alarm clock, as the sun had ruined the extra nine minutes of sleep she could have had. She then padded over to the large, walk-in closet and retrieved Devin's oversized, blue, terry cloth robe with the gold "D" inscribed on the upper, right breast pocket. She had one just like it but preferred to use his, especially after a night of passionate lovemaking. It made her feel closer to him and she savored the sweet memory of him in its folds. Just the scent of his after-shave cologne on the lapel of the robe ignited a fire between her thighs that Taylor knew should have been doused last night.

"We'll just have to take extra measures tonight to make sure the fire is thoroughly quenched," Taylor said mischievously as she admired her taut body in the mirror through the skimpy, see-through nightie. A knock on the door caused her to jump. Cinching the belt of the robe tight around her waist, she opened the bedroom door to find Chaz, her eight-year-old son.

She opened the door wider and by rote, he staggered in, climbed into the center of her bed and was sleeping again within seconds.

Taylor pulled the covers up to his shoulders, kissed his forehead and stared at his sleeping form. His cheeks were still as chubby as when he was a baby, but now, his eyebrows and other distinguishing traits of his father, were now more prominent. His hair was not what would be considered as 'good hair' but a stiff brush would straighten it out completely and then reveal waves that could be traced back to his Indian heritage two to three generations back on his father's side.

Taylor produced a scunci from her vanity dresser and tied it around her shoulder-length, dark brown tresses and into a high ponytail. Although she had a great time last night, she had not slept much and made a mental note that she had not taken a Xanax last night to help her sleep. She left Chaz sleeping and tiptoed down the hall to his brother's bedroom. Devin, Jr. was also still sleeping. Taylor gazed adoringly at her eldest son, who looked like his father's twin. Devin was a cute ten-year-old, who looked thirteen. His hair was silky and straight, only it stayed straight. In fact, he looked like he could have a Spanish mother or father. He was a carmel color, just like Devin, Sr. It was clear that Taylor had simply been used as the vestibule for his birth.

Taylor stroked his hair and he mumbled something in his sleep she couldn't make out.

"My sweet DJ...just like your daddy," she whispered.

She descended the spiral staircase, opting to let the boys sleep another half-hour while she got breakfast started.

Within minutes, the spacious, contemporary, four-bedroom home was filled with the aroma of bacon and scrambled eggs. Taylor heard muffled voices and then footsteps above and knew it was the boys making their way to the bathroom to brush their teeth. Shortly, with a rumble, they appeared, racing to see who could get to the breakfast table first.

"How many times do I have to tell you two about running in the house. Now settle down. Good morning!"

"Good morning. Can I have five pieces of bacon, Ma," DJ asked.

"You're a pig," Chaz shouted and immediately started making snorting noises.

"Shut up before I--"

"Before you what?" Taylor interrupted. You are not his father or mother and if anybody is going to do any disciplining around here, it'll be me. Now, you may have five pieces, if you're that hungry."

"Yeah, you can have five or ten or twenty pieces, pig boy," Chaz managed between a fit of giggles.

"Charles Daniel Harris how would you like to go a week without playing video games?"

Chaz quieted himself immediately.

Taylor served the plates with five strips of bacon for DJ and two for Chaz along with a helping of eggs and a stack of buttered toast.

"Now the two of you eat up and get dressed so that we can be out of here in an hour. I'm going upstairs to take my shower." As she headed up the stairs, she yelled, "And, don't forget to place your dishes in the dishwasher."

Before Taylor could reach the top of the stairs, she could hear DJ and Chaz going at it again.

"I mean it you two," she yelled over the banister. She shook her head and smiled as she closed the door to her bedroom.

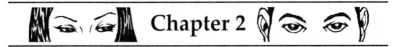

Chapter 2

Taylor maneuvered through the crowded streets of San Francisco in her white, E420 Mercedes. As much as she loved driving her luxury car, if she didn't have to drop the boys off at school, she would surely take public transportation. It seemed like there were more people on the road every day and she hated dealing with it.

"For Pete's sake," she thought aloud. She had a meeting at 8:30 a.m., but at this rate if she didn't make it to the parking garage in the next five minutes she was going to be late. When the light turned green, instead of continuing for another four blocks where she could make a left turn, she made an illegal left turn and was already only a block away from the garage. Her car phone rang. Assuming it was her assistant, Karen, she pressed the hands-free button and spoke.

"I'm coming, Karen."

"Well, if you add my name instead of Karen's it'll sound like a replay of last night," the smooth voice on the other end offered.

Taylor blushed in spite of herself. "Stop it," she admonished her husband.

"I just wanted to say, hi. I had a conference call at 6:00

a.m. this morning with another potential investment group."

"Well why didn't you just make the call from home?"

"I figured I might as well just come into the office. This way I could leave early tonight and Junior can finally be on time to his basketball practice."

"Uh huh," Taylor said distractedly as she pulled into her reserved parking spot. "I think his coach will appreciate that." They both laughed.

"I really just wanted to hear your voice, baby. I realize we've both been so busy that we haven't had time for us and I miss that and...times like last night."

"So do I," Taylor managed as she felt her eyes stinging and the restriction in her throat.

"I'll be home when you get there tonight and don't worry about dinner."

"Thanks Sweetie. Have a good day," she said, stopping in her parking space.

"Taye, you too. Oh, and I love you."

The phone disconnected and Taylor sat for a minute to compose herself. It was true she and Devin had not been together in many months the way they were last night. The distance had begun shortly after Chaz was born. Devin had become distant and withdrawn. She had chalked it up at the time as Devin being between jobs and suddenly having three people who were depending on him. However, she had always been a career woman who contributed to the household both physically and financially.

When Devin's old college friend, Ted Levingston proposed the idea of going into business for himself and Devin becoming a partner, the Devin she had married was back...for a while. There was passion, fire and an endless flow of conversation. Soon he and Ted were traveling all over the country to pitch their idea and gain financial supporters. The next phase of their marriage problems became the lack of time. It seemed there was always something keeping them apart, disconnecting them physically or emotionally. Devin had made good investments that would ensure their income, so they were not hurting for money, which allowed him to travel without worrying about immediate reimbursement of his expenses.

Before either of them knew it, years had passed and their marriage had deteriorated to roommate status--they simply lived under the same roof. Devin stopped making it to the bedroom at all most of last year and before long the family room served as his bedroom. It was then that Taylor fully realized she had to do something. They started marriage counseling a month later and it seemed to be just what they needed to get back on track. Taylor suspected that anyone could have listened to their problems, their parents, their pastor, their friends, but having someone they didn't know who would respect their privacy and hopefully remain objective was key. Three months and $2,400.00 later, they could no longer justify allowing a short Jewish man with a red Afro to sit back and take occasional notes on the lower points of their marriage. Though he had come highly recommended all they had shared over the past several months had been purely notetaking and Taylor was beginning to think that they were going to need to look up another counselor.

But last night a reconnection had been made like when they were newlyweds. There was passion, love, tenderness and an unselfish giving of one to the other and then this morning, the call.

"Maybe there is hope," she whispered, turning off her radio. As she opened the car door, she glanced at her watch and let out a sigh. She was ten minutes late for her meeting.

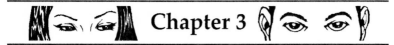 **Chapter 3**

Devin reclined back in his gray, Herman Miller, Aeron mesh chair scanning the rapidly developing landscape from his office in Redwood Shores. The building, in which his company Mymelody.com was housed, was one of the many start-up companies, which had caused real estate properties to soar.

Silicon Valley was big business, creating sixty-four new millionaires a day and Devin was on the fast track to joining this elite group. The website that enabled web browsers to download the latest music singles for free was an instant hit with teenagers and college-aged students allowing them to trade music files over the internet. The first month Mymelody.com's site went public; the site received over 3 million hits. A remarkable feat. Devin had spent the first year of this venture developing a search engine for streaming media and talking with music publishers to strike an alliance and parlay Mymelody.com into the largest fee-based online music service in the world. Under this deal, their little start-up would acquire all the top music artists to their music catalog. And, if they could secure the buy-in from the major music companies such as Sony, EMI and Universal the service would likely become an accepted standard. What remained unclear was just how this new partnership would work. Users used to getting something for nothing might find alternatives that would allow them to swap bootleg music without the need for a central server clearinghouse of the type Mymelody.com provided. Most importantly, they were trying to find ways to work in conjunction with the Recording Industry Association of America (RIAA) to use technology to build artist communities. These obstacles were just the tip of the iceberg.

Devin and Ted's goal was to make or find a way to negotiate the gap between the users trading files for free with the copyright holders who wanted to be paid for their work. So far it had not been mentioned...it was wonderful, but they both knew the obstacles would come. The question was, when?

The vision for Mymelody.com was four-fold with each arrow pointing to the participation of the four major music companies. Most likely if they could get the support of one of the companies, the others would follow. This would give them a lot of legitimacy and enable their way of downloading music as an accepted standard; to get a large venture capital firm behind them, was very close to happening. Lastly, while doing all of this, keep the confidence of customers who swarmed the message boards and chat rooms when they learned that Mymelody.com was going to become more than just an underground resource to fill their bootleg needs. The plan was to become a major player in the industry. It was just a matter of time before everyone came to the Web with the concept of downloading music for money...why shouldn't he and Ted be the first to profit.

Devin leaned back in his chair again and blew out an exasperated breath. The last thing he wanted to do now was travel. They had done so much traveling and selling over the past year and he couldn't wait to get to the "real" nuts and bolts of running his company. He thrived on hiring new talent, enhancing their product and thinking of innovative ways to knock the competition out of the running. Ted on the other hand was a shark and when he smelled blood, he'd go in for the kill. There were days Devin was sure Ted could sell ice to an Eskimo.

If a potential investor had any doubts about their product going into a meeting, Ted would see to it that they didn't at its conclusion. Aggressive in a non-threatening way, Ted was well versed and hungry. As much as Devin didn't want to take another business trip, he knew it was in the company's best interest. The fact is, they needed this venture capital firm to support their efforts and so if it meant schmoozing, then he was going to have to fall in line.

At 6'1 with an athletic build, chiseled features and plenty of cash to throw around, Ted was a magnet for women. He was also a big-time partygoer and ladies man, which in the company of a married man made for a dangerous mix. In this case, the 'Millionaire Men's Club'…middle-aged men, loaded with money and no rules. Many times young female escorts magically appeared right after a business dinner. It was not uncommon to hold a business meeting in the olympic-sized pool in the home of one of the potential investors, where a harem of women offered themselves.

Devin tried to focus his attention back to the PowerPoint presentation on his computer screen. Taylor hated when he traveled and his being gone so much had tested their marriage time and time again. He suspected she knew the types of goings on at these meetings. After all, she worked in the corporate workforce and though not privy to these types of meetings, she knew very well, from other sources, what went on at these off-site meetings.

His thoughts drifted again to the last time he had to tell Taylor he would be gone for four days over a weekend. Her first question was, "Are all your investors single that they hold so many business meetings on weekends?" And her second question was "Or do you just think I'm stupid?"

Taylor knew the kind of guy Ted was...she had heard about all the college stories and failed relationships right down to his leaving his fiancée at the alter. "To his credit, he doesn't have a bunch of bastard children strewn from city to city," she had commented during one of their discussions about Ted. But, she despised him nonetheless and it made for a tense environment each time they had a business meeting at the Harris house. Devin clicked the "file close" button, shut down his computer and headed for the door. This was going to be a long night.

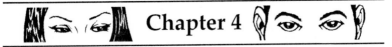

Chapter 4

Taylor zigzagged in and out of traffic, frustrated by the driving habits of the city's drivers. She was exhausted. She was supposed to leave the office by 5:30 p.m. after her 5:00 p.m. meeting that was only supposed to go for half an hour. However, Murphy's Law had been in effect and she didn't leave her office until 5:50 p.m. DJ's basketball practice started at 6:00 p.m. As it turned out, Devin had to work late, so instead of being half an hour late to practice, Taylor and the boys skipped practice altogether. She knew when Frank Sullivan called she should have told him that she was in the middle of something, which would not have been a lie. But, he was the Vice President of Marketing and her peers were her most important clients. Their feedback to their bosses, who interacted with her boss, was critical to her career. Now, as she and the boys pulled into the garage, Taylor looked at the digital display on the car's dashboard. It read 6:56 p.m. She had been late leaving the office, further delayed by snarled traffic and now it was almost 7:00 p.m. With the same routine ever since Chaz was two years old something was going to have to give and soon. She would surely lose her sanity as she had been running on empty. What's more, Devin was never around enough to be of much help. Most times when he came home everything was finished. Dinner was over; dishes put away, the boys were fed, bathed, assisted with their homework and in bed.

Taylor sat staring at the clock that hung on the garage wall. She didn't know what was wrong with her lately. She just felt in such a rut. Sure, last night had been great, but it did not take long for the spell to wear off. She often had to be mother, father, doctor and CFO. Although both she and Devin were making six figures that had not always been the case. She had only been Vice President of Human Resources for two years, which put her salary to low-six figures, but before that she was a director. Devin had been toiling with his start-up for approximately the same amount of time and only up until several months ago, since the company website went public, did he actually begin to see a substantial profit.

It was true that money did not make you happy. She had the money, yet the mortgage on the beautiful home she and Devin owned was eating into them to the tune of $5,100 a month. Of course, this did not include tuition for the boys' private school, car notes and insurance and all the other necessities required to make a home function properly. Expenses were close to $9,000 a month. Taylor shut her eyes and clutched the steering wheel.

"Ma' what's wrong?" DJ asked, concern in his voice. "Why are we still sitting in the car?"

"Yeah, can we leave again and get pizza?" Chaz chimed in.

"No, that's a twenty minute drive to the pizza parlor," Taylor responded as she pulled her key out of the ignition and met her tired gaze in the rear-view mirror. "I'll whip up something quick okay. Maybe tacos?"

"Hooray" Chaz shouted. "Can I have three?"

"Who's the pig boy now?" DJ asked, seizing the opportu

-nity to get back at his younger brother. "Oink, Oink, Oink, Oink, Oink, Oink…" he continued tauntingly.

"Mom, make him stop," Chaz pleaded.

"That's enough you two," Taylor scolded as she opened the car door. "DJ you grow up, that is totally unnecessary. And Chaz maybe you'll remember how being teased by your brother makes you feel when you're teasing him. Now go in the house." The boys filed out of the car and through a door that led them directly into the house.

"I just don't know how long I can do this," Taylor whispered to herself as she retrieved her briefcase from the passenger seat and slowly straightened up inside before exiting her vehicle.

It was 9:45 p.m. and Devin wasn't home yet. Taylor turned off the lamp on her nightstand and tried to get some sleep. She tossed and turned but could not get comfortable. Her mind became flooded with thoughts of her marriage. She and Devin's relationship seemed so tumultuous lately. One day things were fine and the next day they were not.

Just twenty-four hours ago they had enjoyed a rare night of passionate lovemaking, with Devin whispering sweet promises in her ear that her subconscious knew he had no intentions of keeping. Yet, at that moment, her body and heart would have believed he could turn water into wine.

She couldn't understand why this huge disconnect had taken place and began to disrupt the happy marriage they once shared. She had always been extremely attracted to her husband. He was still an extremely handsome man at 6'1 and 210 pounds. Although he jogged every now and again, he wasn't an avid fitness buff, but his body indicated otherwise. He was muscular without being imposing and his light brown eyes were captivating. His short hair was jet-black and straight without the use of chemicals and his skin was the color of melted brown sugar. Her thoughts drifted back to when they were first married and how happy they were. After dating for five years and living together for two of those years, they had no reservations about spending the rest of their lives together. It was funny how things changed.

They had just graduated college a year apart, were living in a studio apartment, working entry-level jobs and were dirt poor. They had to borrow from their parents to pay for the wedding. Even after marriage they struggled for a few years working jobs that didn't allow them to use their degrees.

At one point it was so bad, they had to borrow ten dollars to purchase diapers and formula for Devin Jr. DJ's first couple of years were very lean times for all them. As a human resources representative, employee benefits and HR laws were fascinating, but it didn't pay much. Her boss, a thin, balding man with green eyes and a warm smile had been gracious enough or ignorant enough to allow her to attend any classes that had anything to do with the field of human resources. With a corporation of over 700 people, training was always available, but not always endorsed by supervisors. Therefore, she took full advantage of having a boss that supported her professional development.

Almost a year later, when an HR manager position became available, Taylor jumped at the opportunity to climb the corporate ladder and make more money. She had already taken all the appropriate classes and felt well versed in the area of human resources. She earned the favor of many executives, but it was clearly still a man's world. Often, she found that her White female and male counterparts were earning fifteen to twenty percent more annually. And because bonuses were ten percent of the annual salary, naturally, her bonuses were smaller too, keeping her far behind in the race.

All this only forced Taylor to work harder at being as good as she could be. She held her head high even when she was asked to do the grunt work of scheduling off-site regional meetings for all the senior level human resource staff. There was no way she was going to give them an excuse when an HR Director opportunity presented itself in her department. For three years she worked fifty and sixty hour weeks, often to the point of sheer exhaustion and even some weekends.

Her home life was a mess. Laundry would pile up for weeks before she could get up enough energy or time to wash. She had become so fatigue and forgetful.

Devin couldn't pick up any of the slack because his schedule was worst than hers. He was a manager of business development at an investment company, with just enough flexibility to pick Devin Jr. up from work if he got off early enough to save her the trip. If it had not been for her mother, she would not have been able to get where she was today.

One day, after eating a sandwich for lunch at her desk, she nodded off three separate times. Right then, she decided to call her doctor and see if she could get an emergency appointment to see what was wrong with her. At the very least, she expected to be given some prescription strength vitamins and iron tablets. After urine and blood tests, she almost fell off the examination table when her doctor informed her that she was pregnant and should schedule an appointment with her gynecologist as soon as possible. She drove out of the medical building's parking lot dazed and confused. To this day, she is not sure how she made it home without having a traffic accident.

Her mind raced. She just thought her period was late, not that it wasn't planning to show for the next nine months. They were already struggling. Sure, things had gotten somewhat better with annual increases, but not to the point where another mouth to feed would be easy. She sat on the edge of her bed trying to gather her thoughts. She had about an hour and a half before picking DJ up from her mother's house. He would be starting nursery school in another few months, which would be a new expense. Her mother charged them nothing, but she was a school counselor and would be going back to work herself once the summer was over. Spending time with her first and only grandson was payment enough, she had told them. Taylor patted her flat belly. She had sprung right back into shape after her first pregnancy. She sighed. This certainly did not fall in line with her plans, but this was obviously the way things were meant to be. Abortion was definitely not an option, so she would make Devin's favorite meal and break the news to him after dinner.

Taylor smiled in spite of herself as she lay there thinking about her past...her life. Unfortunately, her mother and father had retired and moved to Phoenix shortly after Chaz was born, leaving her without any back up in terms of watching the boys. She missed her mom and dad. The thought occurred to her that she had not talked to her mother in a couple of weeks. Her mother was the compass that kept her centered. Taylor had deliberately avoided their weekly calls over the past few months because her mother knew her better than anyone. She would surely hone in on any tension she heard in her daughter's voice. Things had worked themselves out, just as she knew this too would pass. Whatever this fugue was that she was in had to just be a phase, but she needed Devin to help her. She was tired of being strong. She wanted to just lean on her husband for once and have him take care of everything.

She was pulled from her reverie by the sound of the garage door opening. Devin was finally home. She straightened the paisley duvet and propped her pillows so as to not give the appearance that she had been laying there for hours, waiting for him.

Within minutes, Devin appeared in the frame of one of the French doors. Taylor could see his silhouette as he walked across the room and placed his briefcase in the walk-in closet. He then removed his suit jacket and loosened his tie. The silence was deafening and when he spoke, it startled her, causing her heart to skip a beat.

"Sorry I'm late, baby. I know I missed picking DJ up for practice. I called the school and obviously you got my message. Just as I was about to leave my office Ted pulled me in on this conference call." He paused and then sighed; "It looks like I'm going to have to go to New York for a few days and talk to some of our investors.

Taylor did not move or acknowledge his presence, but rather lay there wishing that she hadn't heard what he said. She knew he would have to travel soon and she had been dreading this information. Whenever he traveled, they argued and became somehow distanced not only by the miles, but in their marriage as well.

Taylor could not believe how different this night was from last night. She wanted to reach out to her husband and tell him how she felt, that she was losing her grip and him in the process. That she had not forgotten or forgiven his indiscretions and that as a result, her feelings of mistrust had her in a constant state of inner panic, but she still loved him, deeply.

"Taye...are you asleep?" Devin whispered, leaning over her. Taylor remained still, her back to Devin. He paused for a moment, kissed her shoulder and quietly left the room. Taylor lay there in the same position, crying until her pillow became soggy beneath her cheek.

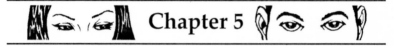 Chapter 5

Devin and Ted landed in New York's LaGuardia Airport anxious and excited. Ted had received a telephone call from a venture capital company that was willing to provide Mymelody.com the capital they needed to help develop a subscription service. The senior vice-president of the company had asked that they fly out a couple of days earlier to meet the company's CEO and that maybe a meeting with Sony could be arranged. They even agreed to pay for first-class hotel accommodations.

"Man this is it, Ted…I just know it! Mymelody's going to be huge," Devin managed over the blaring horns of the New York traffic.

"I know, I know. This is what all the hard work has been about. Yesss!" Ted concluded as he gritted his teeth and threw his fist in the air. A raised brow from the cabby met his actions as he glanced through the rear-view mirror and maneuvered his way through downtown Manhattan to get them to the luxurious Plaza Hotel.

"Yeah, it's pretty sweet!" Devin said, unable to conceal his excitement.

"You bet! And tomorrow is gonna be smooth sailing.

After I give them my best sales pitch and all the reasons why they should invest and take a chance on Mymelody and you then follow up with the numbers and how the system works, they'll be unable to refuse us anything."

"I share your confidence, buddy. But, let's just make sure we're both on top of our game tomorrow. I'm hittin' the bed as soon as we get to the hotel."

"What! You've got to be kiddin' me. This is New York. We need to make the most of it."

"You sound like this is your first time being here. I know you've visited New York alone at least a dozen times."

"That's right and there's still so much to see and so many women to please."

"I hear you, but that flight just wipes me out, man. Not to mention, I'm sure we'll have plenty of time to socialize after our meetings tomorrow."

The cab pulled to a stop in front of the hotel and they made their way through the bustling crowd of New Yorkers and other visiting businessmen. Once they reached the concierge desk, Ted checked them into their respective suites. He handed Devin his room key as they walked over to the bank of elevators. They could have shared a two-bedroom suite, Devin thought, but he knew Ted had intentionally arranged it this way.

Devin pressed the elevator button marked "P" and within minutes they were at the penthouse level. Their suites were across from one another and were two of four on the entire floor. Ted sat his garment bag and suitcase down as he opened the door to his suite.

"If you get restless and decide to have some fun and join me, you know how to get in touch with me."

"I doubt it. Just remember we're losing three hours and our meeting is at 7:30 a.m. tomorrow."

Ted stood wide-legged with his arms out and hands up.

Then, in his best Eddie Murphy impersonation, he said, "Hey, this is my Mac Daddy vibe I'm giving you."

"Okay, Mac Daddy," Devin mocked laughingly. "Enough said."

They both entered their suites and closed the door. Devin placed his luggage on top of the king-sized bed. He was exhausted but he unpacked and took a quick shower to work out some of the stress in his neck and shoulders. Only after his shower did he really start to appreciate how nice his suite actually was. It had a huge bedroom with a sitting area and fireplace. Beyond the bedroom was a living room with a second fireplace, full bar, entertainment center and kitchen. He had to admit it was first-class all the way with Ted.

Devin poured himself a snifter of brandy and relaxed in the sitting area clad in only a bath towel cinched at the waist. He took a sip of the brandy and focused on the crackling fire. After a while, he retrieved his briefcase from the closet. He wanted to make sure he crossed his T's and dotted his I's. As he compared his hard copy handouts with his electronic version, he couldn't help but think about Taylor. He wanted to call her but he knew the conversation would only end up in an argument and he was not prepared to deal with that. He would call her in the morning and let her know he had arrived safely.

After reviewing the documents and feeling confident everything was in order, Devin pulled on a pair of cotton, drawstring pajamas and climbed into bed. The brandy had done its job and relaxed him. Before drifting off, his last thoughts were of his family and how happy he and Taylor used to be.

Devin woke with a start at the sound of the telephone ringing for his wake-up call.

He reached over, picked up the receiver and listened to the recorded message, then hung up the phone without waiting for the message to end. He sat up on his elbows and glanced at the clock on the nightstand. It was 5:30 a.m., which meant it was 2:30 a.m. at home. Taylor would be in a deep sleep as usual. He dismissed it as her adjusting to her new role as Vice-President of Human Resources. It was clear that the transition had been tough and not made any easier with his already hectic schedule.

He walked over to the closet and chose the suit he would wear today. A navy blue cashmere and wool blend with a white dress shirt and pale yellow, silk tie.

Devin showered, ordered a continental breakfast from room service and while waiting for the bellman dialed his home number. After four rings he heard Taylor's voice on the other end.

"Hello," she answered groggily.

"Good morning," Devin responded.

"Good morning?" Taylor asked, clearing her throat. "Devin, it's 2:30 in the morning."

There was a pause.

"Yeah, I just wanted to let you know I'm situated. I would have..."

"Wait a minute," Taylor interrupted. She propped herself up on one elbow and turned on the lamp which sat atop the night stand. "Amazing. You know with modem technology there is no reason that you could not have called me...cell phone, pay phone, hotel phone...I'm sure at least one was at your disposal. It would not have killed you to call and say you had arrived safely. You have a family here, but you have no regard for anyone's feelings other than your own."

"Look Taylor, what do you want me to say? You're right, okay. I was just beat by the time we made it to the hotel."

"I just bet you were. Because you probably didn't go

straight to the hotel to begin with. And I'm sure if Ted had any-thing to do with it, you wouldn't be able to call me now."

Devin sighed. "Don't start. Just don't start."

"What do you mean don't start. See that's the other prob-lem. I realize he's your partner and everything, but you take his side over mine and I'm your wife."

"You know what? I didn't call you for this. That's why I didn't call last night…I just didn't have the energy for this and I don't have it now either. When are you going to get off this kick?"

"When you wake up and realize that your partner is noth-ing more than a whore who is destroying your marriage because he has never had a committed relationship and wouldn't know one if it came up to him and slapped him."

"Do you know how immature you sound? Huh? I just wish…"

"Immature!" Taylor interjected. "You know what? This conversation is over."

Taylor hung up the phone and Devin sat rooted to his chair with the phone still to his ear. He was not at all surprised by the outcome of his conversation with his wife. In actuality, he was more pissed off than he had been in a long time. She didn't even bother to ask his room number, although she could get the information from his secretary, it was just the point that she shouldn't have to. In his mind, if they had better communica-tion, he would have provided those details to her before he left.

He finished his breakfast and got dressed with still an hour to go before their meeting. He was anxious and tense because of his unhappy resolution to his call with Taylor. If he had followed his first mind, he would not have called her until he was in the airport on his way home. There was a knock on the door and Devin was grateful for the distraction from his evil, meandering thoughts.

Devin opened up the door and it was Ted. He was surprised to see him on time and prepared. It was definitely not the norm.

"Hey buddy...let's do this!"

"All right! What'd you strike out last night? You're here way too early."

"Quite the contrary my man. Quite the contrary. It's just that, clearly I understand my priorities. I mean, I haven't ran into a piece yet that would make me miss putting money in my pocket."

They both laughed. Devin grabbed his briefcase and they headed out the door.

"You are definitely the man, Dev," Ted rambled as they unwound in a bar overlooking the Manhattan skyline.

"Oh, but I been tryin' to tell you that for years now," Devin gloated, engaging his friend in their boastful exchange.

"I mean what we pulled off in that meeting was pure genius. By the time we left there we could have asked for anything we wanted and they would have said yes."

"That's the truth man. That's the truth."

"I mean I started to ask for a Bentley while I was up in there, 'ya know what I'm sayin'?" Ted joked, putting on his bad boy routine.

"Job well done! You are one silver-tongued devil if I do say so myself, my brotha," Devin joked, playing along with his partner.

"Seriously though, man. You sold the idea of using technology to build artist communities," Devin said, changing the mood of the conversation. "That went over very well with those bigshots."

"Coupled with the fact that the software was developed to save users the time consuming effort of wading through site after site to find a particular artist. Your demonstration was the key selling point," Ted countered.

"Yeah, it was definitely a good meeting," Devin concurred.

"Wow, look at the time. It's already after four o'clock. We have just enough time to get back to the hotel, get changed and meet Craig and Pete for dinner at their company condo."

Dinner was served at promptly at 7:45 p.m. in the formal dining room of the Ion Venture Capital Investment Firm's condo, usually reserved for high-profile clients visiting from out of state. The condo came with maid service and an on-call chef. Of course, chauffer service was another additional perk of doing business with this firm. The dinner was an excellent presentation of seafood fit for a king and dessert was as entertaining to the eye as it was delicious to the palate with cherries jubilee flambéed at the table. Both Ted and Devin were in good spirits, having had drinks a few hours earlier, cocktails before dinner and now after dinner cocktails. It was an environment where you didn't say 'no'.

"Now for a tour of the condo gentlemen, where you both are welcome to stay for the last night of your trip. Our meetings aren't until 9:00 a.m. tomorrow morning...late by New York standards and just a formality," Craig Childress, senior partner of the firm joked. Devin was amazed that this fellow was already senior partner and was probably five years younger than he. He had to be somebody's nephew or something, he thought.

The other executive, Peter Cavanaugh, who may have been Devin's age, chimed in,

"Yeah fellas, your last night in New York should be spent in style."

"Pete, Craig...I agree," Ted relented, which came as no surprise to Devin. Although the only other plan for the evening was the tour of the condo, Devin suspected there was something more to this visit.

The house was the most exquisite condo Devin had ever laid eyes upon...even on some of those home shows Taylor watched now and then. The tri-level condominium had four master suites with private baths attached plus two additional bathrooms, a large gourmet kitchen on the main level with another small, though fully-equipped kitchen on the second level. In the condominium there was a den, wine cellar, mini movie theatre and last but not least, a club with a DJ, full bar and bartender on the top, third level.

As the four gentlemen stepped off the elevator, Devin became aware that there was no distinction between this environment and any other men's club he had ever attended under the guise of 'doing business'.

"Ooh wheeeeee! Pete, Craig, it's about to get thick in here," Ted shouted above the music, echoing what was already on Devin's mind.

"As we said before, we thought you gentlemen's last night in New York should be spent in style," Pete offered.

Devin's mind reeled as the music reached a deafening crescendo. There were at least twelve women lined up and waiting, which according to his count would be three women per man. Some of the women danced with each other, some wound their bodies around poles and others just stood...waiting. He did not want to be there. In fact, he would rather be anyplace else but where he was right now. Even in his alcohol induced haze he knew that.

Devin glanced toward the bar where condoms were laid

out like pretzels.

"I think I should go back to the hotel room and sleep this off," Devin managed.

"Come on, man," Ted said, putting his arm around Devin's shoulder, whispering urgently in his ear. "I know this is probably uncomfortable for you, but our colleagues would be insulted. Not good for business, if you know what I mean. I'm not tryin' to pressure you to do anything but to stay and put up a good front. Our business depends on it. I mean think about it. Have you ever known potential investors to go to all this trouble for some tiny company such as this? We're not a couple of rich Arabs or oil tycoons. But, they see the huge potential for this...they see money, so it's nothing for them to shell out a little money because the returns will be great."

Devin knew that as sick as it was, Ted was right. He didn't want to be the one who lost Mymelody the funding it needed because he couldn't 'play the game.'

"Yeah man...yeah," he agreed solemnly.

"Aaaawright. This is gonna pay off for us. You'll see," Ted rattled on as he honed in on an Asian woman dancing seductively in the corner and staring straight at him. Pete and Craig were already receiving lap dances and enjoying themselves immensely. From out of nowhere, a stunningly beautiful, brunette with an hourglass figure, took Devin by the hand and led him to another dimly lit corner of the room. He did not resist, what was worst was that he didn't want to. He wanted to lose himself in the moment and wake up when it was over. The brunette never spoke a word, never bothered to ask his name. However, they communicated through eye contact and she seemed to know that she had full reign to do what she wanted...and she did.

After some teasing and foreplay, Devin was enthralled in her web as she rode and straddled him mercilessly. She then backed off, knowing that she had him where she wanted him. She led him to the elevator and to the first floor of the condo and then ultimately to one of the master suites...never saying a word. When she closed the door behind them and stretched out on the bed, it was Devin's turn to take a ride.

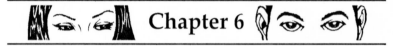 **Chapter 6**

Taylor sat at her desk with her door closed rubbing her temples. She had been trying to get rid of her headache since her conversation with Devin this morning.

How dare he not call me when he got in last night, she thought. Odds were good that Ted had convinced him to go out to some club or do something that they both shouldn't be doing.

What really grated her nerves was that Devin always had a very convenient excuse...too convenient for her liking. Everything was business, according to him. It wasn't that she doubted that many of the meetings and trips were legitimate, but she knew that very little business could be going on at the hours Devin proposed meetings were happening.

She wanted to trust Devin, but his indiscretions over the years had made that near impossible. Even with hard proof like names, photos and actual sitings, her woman's intuition and his attitude confirming she was on point in her assumptions, she still needed the smoking gun.

Taylor had always hoped that it would just run its course and Devin would mature or get tired and recognize the error of his ways. Most importantly, she hoped he would realize how dangerous infidelity could be. AIDS was real. In a nutshell, he risked both their lives with his irresponsible behavior.

As far as she could surmise, she was still waiting for Devin to wake up and get some sense. She opened the drawer to her desk and retrieved a bottle of Excedrin, took two tablets and washed it down with some of the bottled water that sat upon her desk. All of this was getting old. She was so tired of putting up fronts to her parents and family, in-laws and friends. Everybody just assumed that Devin and Taylor Harris were living the American Dream. In actuality, they were farther from it than anyone she knew. Her line buzzed, invading her thoughts.

"Diane is here to see you."

"Tell her I'll be with her in just a few minutes."

Taylor checked her Palm Pilot and noted that this was her last meeting of the day. She pulled the personnel file and briefly reviewed it. Apparently, Diane had a situation in her department that she didn't know how to handle. An employee she supervised had been distributing pornographic emails throughout the department and it had gotten back to her.

Taylor opened her door and Diane was standing right there waiting.

"Hi Diane, come on in. I'll be with you in just a sec."

Taylor walked out to Karen's desk and asked that she hold all of her calls and to only interrupt her if Devin called.

"Sure thing."

Taylor walked into her office and closed the door behind her to a waiting Diane.

"Thanks for squeezing me in today, Taylor. I really appreciate it. You got my voicemail, right?"

"Yes, I did," Taylor responded, still battling the headache that had made its way from her temples to behind her eyes. She really liked Diane. They did lunch every now and again, but Taylor was really not in the mood to talk to anyone today.

"I've pulled Rosalind Perez's personnel file," Taylor said

passing it to Diane,

"And with the exception of this incident, she seems to be an employee in good standing with the company. Been with us for almost four years, has received very good annual reviews...even from you ten months ago. So, the best way to proceed with this is to sit her down and explain to her that you are giving her a verbal warning. Outline the policies and procedures, surrounding misuse of company equipment. Give her a copy of the handbook if you need to, that way she won't be able to say she didn't know."

"And what if this continues?" Diane asked nervously. "You see Taylor, I just don't want to deal with this anymore."

"I beg your pardon. Diane, did I miss something? As I said, her personnel file looks fine."

"I know, but Rosalind has worked for me almost two years, and for almost the past year, she has been consistently late to work, she stays on personal phone calls and I'm convinced that at least half the work she does on her computer is not work-related."

Taylor shook her head in astonishment. She could not believe how in the dark this woman was. These were the types of situations that made her job difficult. After almost a year of going through this with her employee, Diane now wanted immediate results and unfortunately, HR just did not work that way.

"Well, you can't just go back to your office and fire her for something she's been doing for a year with no reprimand. There has to be a paper trail established to substantiate your actions. Right now, there is nothing in her file to indicate that she has been anything other than an upstanding employee."

Diane looked off into space and soon her eyes began to well up with tears. "I just can't deal with this Taylor," she managed between sobs.

Taylor was shocked by this outburst. She reached in her drawer and retrieved a couple of tissues for Diane.

"Deal with what?" Taylor asked, astonished.

"There's just so much going on in my personal life right now and I just don't need this," Diane rambled. "My husband just filed for divorce and my life is a mess...I just can't deal with this right now, Taylor."

Taylor sensed there was something amiss, but she wasn't prepared for this type of confession. She rose and knelt at Diane's side, placing her arm supportively around her shoulder. This was the complicated part of her job. She had her own marriage problems to deal with and certainly was not in a position to advise anyone else on matters of the heart.

"Diane, it'll be okay. Maybe you should take some time off and clear your head. I'm sure it will make this a small matter and you'll be better able to deal with it," Taylor offered, side-stepping the personal issue of Diane's marriage.

"No! I can't do that, I've been off too much already and as a result I'm behind on several projects."

"Diane, I think we need to bring the focus back to the matter at hand," Taylor said as she stood, hoping Diane would get the hint and begin to wrap this up. "I really do sympathize with you, but you must pull it together. As Rosalind's manager, if you want this issue resolved you must communicate to her that what she is doing is inappropriate. With this, you can establish a paper trail. If her attendance is an issue, you can place her on a sixty or ninety day performance program with specific guidelines. If the guidelines are not met, that could count as a second warning."

Diane. had regained her composure and sat glaring, puffy-eyed at Taylor.

"You know, you're right," she said, as if hearing Taylor for the first time. "I just need to get it together," Diane said, dabbing at her eyes. "What should I do next?" she asked eagerly.

"Just sit down with her and in a clear, calm and concise manner, explain to her the rules. What time she should be at work and to limit her personal phone calls to a minimum. You can make the determination as to whether you want this warning to go in her personnel file or not. But, all conversations from this point on should be documented.

Diane took notes as if her life depended on it. Taylor suspected that Diane had come to some understanding about more than her employee during the course of their meeting. She was glad someone had.

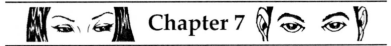 **Chapter 7**

Devin awoke at 5:43 a.m. on Tuesday morning feeling surprisingly little guilt after his reservations about last night.

The brunette whom he had succumbed to last night lay sleeping soundly at his side. He rolled away from her in disgust. If they had been in his hotel room, he would have told her to get up and get out.

His priority now was getting back to the hotel to get showered and changed for he and Ted's 9:00 a.m. meeting at the Twin Towers. But first, he had to find Ted.

He got out of bed and hurriedly put on his slacks and socks. He then found his shoes, shirt and jacket and made his way out of the bedroom. He went to the kitchen to finish dressing before looking for his partner, but Ted was already there, fully dressed and sitting at the table drinking a glass of orange juice.

"Man, I was 'gonna give you ten more minutes before I came looking for you. Some night last night, huh? This is livin," Ted went on without pausing.

"Yeah, some night. Where are Pete and Craig?" Devin asked, not wanting to engage his friend in this conversation.

"Who knows? They're grown men...I'm sure they'll find

their way to the meeting today."

"You're right...let's get outta here and get ready for our meeting."

"No sweat. You know this is in the bag. All we have to do is show up."

"I don't want to take anything for granted. Until we see the money in our account, I'm operating business as usual. And, we still have to get through lunch."

"Yeah, but it's at Windows on the World. That's one of the top restaurants, if not the top restaurant in New York."

"I hear you, man. But let's wait before we start counting our chickens."

Devin and Ted hopped a cab and went back to their hotel. Within the hour, they were packed and prepared to have their last meeting before flying back to San Francisco. By 8:00 a.m., the two were meeting in the hotel's restaurant to go over some last minute details. After concluding that everything was in order and that this meeting would be fairly low-key just to reiterate yesterday's meeting, Ted paid the check and began walking down Fifth Avenue. The air was cool, but the day was unusually beautiful. New Yorkers hustled to and fro, making their way through the crowded Vesey and West Streets. When Devin and Ted had only made it a block from the restaurant, Ted realized he had forgotten his Palm Pilot organizer.

"Aaaw man, I gotta go back to the restaurant. You know I live by that thing!" Ted exclaimed. "I'll be screwed up for days if I don't get it back."

Mildly annoyed, Devin checked his watch. It was 8:39 a.m. "Not good, man...not good," he admonished.

"Look, why don't you go ahead and I'll catch up with you," Ted offered.

"No. We go together...as a team or else it appears that we don't have our stuff together."

The two men walked hurriedly back to the restaurant. Ted walked in just as the waitress was about to hand the Palm Pilot to a gentleman Ted had noticed earlier in the restaurant and presumed him to be the manager.

"I was just coming back for that," Ted said, gesturing to the leather-encased computer.

"Absolutely, sir. I'm glad you came back for it," the waitress responded, flashing Ted a knowing smile. She handed Ted the Palm Pilot and he handed her a twenty-dollar bill.

"Thank you," she said, smiling seductively.

"No, thank you. This is invaluable to me." With that, Ted and Devin left the restaurant once again.

"You know, I don't know what women see in your ugly mug," Devin joked, feeling relieved that Ted had found his Palm Pilot and it hadn't required much time. At this rate, they would still arrive early for their meeting, which always made a good impression.

Ted opened the leather flap on the case of his Palm Pilot and was not surprised to find a small, white piece of paper that appeared to have been ripped from a receipt book. On it was a telephone number and the name Leslie scrawled neatly on the paper.

"You see, there are two types of men in this world...there's me and then there's everybody else! And," Ted continued with an air of confidence, "It's just 8:46...we've still got fourteen minutes to spare."

Both men laughed out loud as they walked briskly toward their destination, some three blocks away.

Suddenly, as if it were happening in slow motion, Devin noticed an airplane slam into one of the Twin Towers. The entire city must have noticed it at the same time, as all sound seemed to stop. The air was thick with disbelief. Even the sounds of traffic seemed silenced by this unbelievable occurrence.

Devin and Ted stood rooted in the middle of the street. The sound seemed to have been turned back on and Devin could hear collective sighs and screams. People began pulling out their cell phones calling friends and loved ones.

"What in the hell!" Ted managed.

The two men did not know what to do, so they stood and watched in horror as their world crumbled before their eyes.

As if imploding in slow motion, one of the Twin Towers began to crumble and fall. People who only minutes ago had been rooted in place at the sight of an airplane slamming into one of the towers now had the horrible displeasure of witnessing a second plane plow into the second tower. Reality began to sink into minds frozen in terror. It was real now. People ran for their lives. The city was ablaze amid the mass panic and cacophony. Devin realized the sound was so loud it was deafening. With New York's rich diversity and multi-lingual culture, at this moment, everyone spoke the same language…fear.

Devin and Ted turned on their heels and fell in step with the oncoming crowd. They ran seeking shelter anywhere and everywhere, but it was not to be found. Hundreds of people including police officers ran down the middle of the street until they could no longer feel building debris pelting their backs. Many people were covered in dust, as if they had been rolled in flour. The falling debris had injured others. Their blood was such a stark contrast to the gray soot and dust that they looked like wounded extraterrestrials from a sci-fi movie.

Many of the elderly, children and women were trampled. Devin set his sights on an elderly woman who had fallen. Several people fell over the woman. The fear and confusion of the crowd was unforgiving. In their panic, no one in the crowd ever bothered to help the injured.

"Man, what is going on here?" Ted yelled to be heard above the roar of the crowd. They raced down the street clutching their briefcases in a death grip.

Devin was slightly ahead of Ted but had still been able to see him out of his peripheral. But when he looked for him on his right to respond, he noticed Ted was not there. There were so many people he could not slow to stop or turn around in search of his friend. The crowd had separated them.

He struggled against the oncoming crowd, keeping sight of the fallen woman. When he reached her, he lifted her to her feet and helped her along the side of the concourse. Just before making it to Church Street, one of the plane's engines fell, crashing into the pavement in front of them. Amazingly, no one had been hit by it.

"I need to rest son," the elderly lady managed. "I can't go any more. My leg," she winced in pain.

Devin had not noticed the gaping wound in the woman's leg. He was surprised at how well she had done all this time. She needed medical attention soon. Gingerly he eased the woman down on the curb and used his tie as a tourniquet to stop the bleeding.

"Thank you. Go on now, I'll be all right. I hear ambulances and fire trucks. I'll get some medical help soon."

"Are you sure?" Devin inquired, feeling horrible about leaving the woman, but there was no way he could carry her to the nearest hospital.

"I'm sure. We have New York's finest here," she said, shooing Devin away.

His first thought was to head for the hotel, but he was unsure of the stability and safety of any building right now.

As he ran, unsure of exactly where to go, he pressed the speed dial button on his cellular phone to call his wife.

"Man, the line is busy."

In times of crisis, the phone was the first thing people went for. Although he had not totally grasped the concept of what was happening, he knew the act was hostile. He had never been in the military, but he was certain this was war.

The crowd slowed down. Devin could only hope that maybe he was at a safe distance. He soon realized why the crowd had slowed and gasped in bewilderment. Both Towers were on fire while thick, black smoke could be seen from every angle. The Tower of the World Trade Center collapsed as if it had been a scheduled implosion of a condemned building. Two people jumped out of their office windows as the crowd looked on in horror. Devin could not ascertain whether firefighters were close enough to catch these people or not. He gauged that these people were between the 101st and 110th stories of the building. No one could catch them from that distance.

Devin's stomach coiled in knots at the sight. But even more disturbing was the third person that jumped from the building...a man in a suit. Devin could not make out his ethnicity or even the exact color of his suit. He only knew that this man had made peace with himself and with his Maker. His form was beautiful...almost elegant, as if being rated on his diving performance by a group of judges at a swimming competition.

He dove headfirst into the air and then spread his arms out at his sides, like a gliding bird high above the clouds. His tie, light in color, billowed angelically out in front of him. His form would have rated the highest score. The crowd watched until he disappeared behind some other buildings. Devin was thankful that he had not been close enough to see his final descent. The silence was deafening. Devin stopped breathing. How horrible must it have been inside that building to make jumping seem like the better option? There was too much left to his imagination and he felt bile rise in his throat. He turned away, tears glisten

-ing on his ashen cheeks.   His own mortality had been challenged and he knew his life had changed forever.

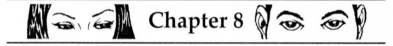 **Chapter 8**

The alarm sounded at 5:00 a.m. on Tuesday morning. Taylor hit the snooze button and continued to lie there. She had taken a couple of sleeping pills last night to help her rest. She could not remember the last time she slept so soundly. Normally, she might wake at some point during the night to use the restroom and check on the boys, but not last night. Her sleep had been deep, dreamless and restful. She suspected if her bladder had filled to capacity during the night, she might have awaked cold and wet for nothing short of the house collapsing was going to disturb her.

At 5:30 a.m. Taylor reached for the remote and turned on the morning news. She had no intention of going to work today…she just could not force herself to do it. Sure, there were a couple of meetings scheduled on her calendar today, but she would call later and have Karen reschedule them. For now, she would have a leisurely morning, take the boys to school, come back home and go to sleep. Maybe she would take another sleeping pill when she returned so that she could totally relax.

Her thoughts drifted back to her last conversation with Devin. It made her head throb just thinking about it. No matter what they promised one another, in the end, the arguing persist

41

-ed. As she reflected, there was no question what the root of their problems were. Yet, neither of them seemed willing to admit it. The fact was that Ted was not the type of person any married woman would want her husband around, even if she were able to keep her eyes on them at all times. She dared to call him a friend to Devin because a friend would be mindful of family and would not have her husband traipsing off from state to state. Neither Devin nor Ted seemed to realize that Devin was a married man with two sons to help raise.

She was just so tired of the emotional roller coaster that camouflaged as her marriage. Why was it so hard for Devin to do the right thing? And more importantly, what was it going to take for him to realize how fortunate he was to live the life he led. The news had been turned down low, but the words 'New York' caused Taylor to actually look at the television and adjust the volume slightly higher.

Although the volume had been turned up, Taylor focused not on what was being said, but the picture of the New York City's Twin Towers. She knew Devin had a meeting in that area, but had no idea at what time. It was not uncommon for the news to show the Twin Towers when referring to something that might have an affect on the economy, the stock market or some millionaire mogul who worked there in one of the skyscraper buildings. As she looked on at the taped footage, she flinched as though she had been slapped, as a plane seemed to expertly maneuver itself into the side of one of the Towers. Taylor could not believe her eyes. She tried to convince herself that this was some Hollywood stunt that the media had taken a particular interest in. But, when she noticed yet a second plane slam into the other Tower, her breath caught in her throat. She groped for the remote control, not realizing that she had dropped it. Unable to manipulate the television volume quickly enough, she scurried out of bed and turned the volume up manually. The news anchors looked distraught, when the programming tuned back to the studio.

"Once again, two jets have slammed into New York City's Twin Towers and the Pentagon in Washington...the President has been evacuated and taken to a safe location." The newscaster reported, a note of hysteria evident in his cracking voice.

It was real. Taylor jumped out of bed and began pacing in front of the television. She could not fathom what she had just seen. Further, what did it mean? Was the world coming to an end? Too many times she had heard her grandparents and mother talk about living in the last days, but this surely had to be that day and it was surreal to her that she was experiencing this type of horror. She felt totally trapped, helpless, scared and uncertain of what to do next. Was she having a mental breakdown?

She stopped pacing and glared at the tube as one of the still burning Towers collapsed. Taylor stood rooted to the floor, horrified. Without thinking, she reached for the phone and began dialing Devin's cell phone number. She was greeted by a recorded message: "All circuits are busy...please try your call again."

With badly shaking hands, she punched in the number again, only to be greeted by the same message. She sat on the edge of the bed, unable to breathe or think...tears brimming in her eyes. Suddenly, there was quick knock and the door to her bedroom opened and in walked both of her sons.

"What are both of you doing up so early?" Taylor asked wiping her eyes.

"We couldn't sleep no more?" Chaz said groggily

"Okay," Taylor said, kissing each of her sons on the forehead. "Well, why don't you both get washed up and I'll be down in a minute."

Taylor put on her robe and tried to blink back the tears.

43

"Are we going to school today?" DJ asked.

"I'm not sure yet, mommy's not feeling too well today," Taylor explained. She turned the volume down but her eyes remained focused on the television.

"Is that why you're crying?" asked DJ. He had always been very mature for his age, but his intuitiveness was remarkable at times. She almost wanted to explain to him what she had just witnessed and her fear, but she knew it was her job to be strong. She knew she was jumping to conclusions at this point. She just had to be. The fact was that she was the adult here and it was important that she acted as such.

"Yeah, that's why. I just need a few minutes. Why don't you boys go and brush your teeth and put on your clothes. I'll be out in a few minutes to make your breakfast."

Chaz had already situated himself beneath the covers in his usual spot in the center of her bed. With some reluctance, he slowly rolled out of bed and made his way over to the door by his brother. DJ looked back at her with uncertainty.

"I'm okay, baby...really. Go on now."

With that, he eased the door closed behind them. She could hear them running down the hall to their bathroom. She would normally scold them for running in the house, but today it was just not important. She turned the volume back up on the television, unable to take her eyes from the television screen as she clutched the phone. Her mind raced with all sorts of horrible possibilities and while she did not know exactly where Devin's meeting was, she had the sinking feeling that it was either in The World Trade Center or somewhere very close to it.

She popped another sleeping pill into her mouth to calm her nerves. What was she going to do? It was too early on the West Coast to reach anyone. She hated to do it, but she needed desperately to talk to someone. She picked up the receiver again and punched in her friend, Camara's number.

The phone rang only once before being answered.

"Hello Camara? I'm sorry to wake you so early, but something horrible has happened and..." Taylor rambled apologetically.

"Oh my goodness. You don't have to apologize. I was already up because my brother just happened to call me this morning before going to work. He wanted me to help his fiancée with their wedding plans. Half an hour later, I'm coming from the bathroom and I hear on the television about this horrible plane crash."

"Camara, I am so scared. Devin is in New York too and I can't reach him on his cell phone. I've been trying ever since I saw the crash on the news. I just don't know what to think," Taylor spoke as she paced the floor. Tears begin to well up in her eyes again.

"Look, it's not going to do either of us any good to be alone. I'm coming over and we'll watch and wait together until we hear something...some good news. We can't assume the worst just yet."

"I-I hope you're right," Taylor managed between sniffles.

"I've got to be strong for the boys, but I can't help but think the worst. Things have been so weird lately."

Both women sighed. "Give me half an hour and I'll be right over," Camara offered.

Taylor hung up the phone, glad that she'd called her friend. Taylor and Camara had been friends since Spelman College. Spelmanites to the end. The interesting thing about their friendship was how parallel their lives were, but with a twist. Both had majored in Business Administration in college. However, Taylor had opted to apply hers to human resources and Camara was applying hers to her own successful public relations firm.

In college, they dated the same type of men. In fact,

Taylor was supposed to go out on a blind date, set up by another classmate, with John Wells. But, at the last minute chickened out and made it a point not to be there.

Camara being her usual curious self, wanted to see what Taylor's blind date looked like, so she posed as her best friend.

When John arrived, Camara was immediately smitten. He was definitely more her type than he was Taylor's. He was every woman's dream if you liked the linebacker type. John Wells was six foot two, two hundred ninety pounds and had hands the size of Cadillac rims. He was huge but well groomed and light on his feet for such a big man. If there were three different shades of black, he was blacker, blackest and purple. Teeth as white as the driven snow commanded attention to his face, where one would be rewarded by warm, caring eyes.

Camara and John dated through college and three years later got married. John wanted a son more than anything in the world. But, after four unexplained miscarriages, they both decided it just was not meant to be.

Adoption was not something either of them wanted. John wanted a son or daughter of his own. Camara had a tubiligation and resigned herself to the fact that her path had been chosen.

Over the years, Camara and John grew distant. John's job as a sports agent kept him away for weeks at a time negotiating contracts for his athlete clients. His love for the game of football and any sport made time fly for him when away from his wife. He had blown out his knee in his junior year of college, ending a promising career before it ever began. For John, becoming a sports agent was the next best thing to being a football player.

On one of his trips that would end in Atlanta before coming back home, Camara decided to meet John at the airport. Excited and extremely horny after not seeing her husband for almost two weeks, Camara checked the flight schedule to make sure John's flight had arrived on time. It had. She ran to gate number twenty-three to surprise her husband as soon as he disembarked the plane.

Camara made it there just moments before the passengers disembarked at Gate 23. She stood there waiting anxiously in a black trench coat and pumps. Beneath her coat, she wore a newly purchased pair of sexy, black, lace and velvet panties with a matching bra. Her loins were an inferno with flames that only her husband could quench.

As people continued to off-board the plane, Camara moved over to the side and out of the way of people greeting their loved ones.

She thought she heard John's voice muffled with footsteps up the walkway. It was probably some passenger he had met on the plane who had taken an interest in what John did for a living.

Just as Camara was about to take a few steps forward and call his name, John appeared. He was not alone. Camara's attention was immediately drawn to her husband's hand that was interwoven with a woman ten years his junior, svelte and blond. With her heart beating double time and mouth as dry as sandpaper, Camara took a few steps back in disbelief.

John did not immediately see her, but when he did, he released the young woman's hand and headed towards his wife. Camara looked for an exit, any exit that would get her out of the airport and away from the image that would haunt her forever.

When John finally caught up with Camara, she had made her way to the curb where her rental car was illegally parked.

"Wait up Camara would you please?"

"Wait for what John, huh? Camara asked not waiting for a reply. "You go straight to hell!" Her hands shook so badly she could barely get her key in the door's lock.

"At least let me explain, Cammie," John pleaded.

Camara made her way into the car and behind the steering wheel. She looked her husband straight in the eye. "John, if you had a legitimate excuse, you wouldn't have chased me through the airport. I just wish you'd been man enough to let me know where I stood."

John stood there with his mouth gaping open, but producing no sound. He was shocked by the entire incident, but more so by the way his wife was handling things.

A simple, "I'm sorry," was all he could manage.

"John, the next time you hear from me, it'll be through my attorney. I hope she was worth it!" Camara put her car in drive and sped off, signifying the end of their marriage.

Taylor reflected on her best friend's divorce. She and Camara had sat up all night on the phone crying. Taylor consoled her friend as best she could. Now, it seemed her marriage was headed in the same direction, but being cut off from her husband and not knowing his fate, seemed to put things into perspective.

She wanted so badly to talk to Devin and tell him how much she loved him...words she should have spoken long ago. Now, she could only wait and hope that it was not too late.

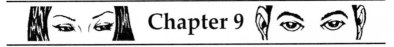

Chapter 9

Ted had become separated from Devin. There were just so many people. Adults, children, the elderly. Everybody looked alike...scared and confused. He was no different. Having been to New York several times since January, he was no stranger to getting around the city, but today was like a modern-day Armageddon. It reminded him of some old footage he'd seen once on Hitler's reign of terror. The buildings had been bombed and people ran for their lives with no real destination, except to seek safety.

Ted scanned the sea of people, looking for Devin. All methods of communication were out. Ted continued to walk aimlessly. For the first time in his life, he was not in control, uncertain of what to do next. The crowd of people moved him forward. As he walked past a building, he caught a glimpse of someone. His clothes were disheveled and covered in ash and he clutched a briefcase in his arms. Face gray with debris, Ted stepped closer to get a better look. As he approached, he noticed that this figure was moving in sync with him. They both clutched their briefcases. Ted approached the mirrored building and pressed his hand against the hand of the image staring back at him.

Even in his darkest hour and in the midst of a near death experience, his primary focus was on money. What did he have to show for all his hard work? A beautiful condominium, a nice car and a bevy of women. He had never been the marrying kind and he was okay with that. Many men would kill to have his life. But the image that stared back at him was a coward...scared and clutching documents that could potentially make him a millionaire ten times over.

With a new resolve, Ted reached in his breast pocket and extracted a handkerchief. He wiped his face, patted his hair and carried the briefcase confidently in his right hand. Yes, what had just happened was a tragedy. Two planes crashing into the World Trade Center Towers was certainly going to have an affect on the U.S. economy.

He tried his secretary at the office, but the phone lines were still busy.

"Great," He hissed to himself.

First order of business was to get a plane back to San Francisco and start making some calls to his investors. He had to make sure that this incident would not scare them so badly that they would not want to invest their money in Mymelody.com.

Devin needed to listen to the news to make sure there had been no attacks on San Francisco.

"We're live near the scene of The World Trade Centers where America has come under attack. At 8:46 this morning, an airplane slammed into The World Trade Centers followed by a second plane and a third crashing into the Pentagon."

Devin's mouth dropped open. This can not be happening, he thought. The Pentagon was the backbone of our country. If someone had gotten close enough to breach that type of security, what was next?

"Currently a wing of the Pentagon is on fire. The scene is surreal. We have no word yet on casualties, but we can assume the loss of life will be profound.

The second Tower of the World Trade Center just collapsed. I repeat; the second Tower of the World Trade Center has just collapsed. Both of the Twin Towers are no longer. The New York skyline will never be the same..."

This had taken his fear and anxiety to a new level. He turned on his heels with a renewed determination.

"I've got to get back home to my family."

It was 4:17 p.m. Eastern Standard Time and Devin had just received the okay, along with hundreds of other guests, that the hotel was safe enough for them to go in and retrieve their items.

"You mean we gotta find anotha hotel to stay at? " One middle-aged man with a Boston accent asked.

"I'm sorry, but yes. The Fire Marshall has given all businesses in the area one hour to evacuate," the perky brunette offered apologetically.

"The service elevators will be running for the upper

floors and floors 1-10, unless handicapped or otherwise incapacitated, will need to use the stairwell.

"This is absurd," another senior gentleman added. He reminded Devin of Thurston Howell, III from Gilligan's Island.

"Well can we get this show on the road for cryin' out loud," someone else asked impatiently.

Devin recognized the voice and turned in the direction of the stares of the crowd. He maneuvered his way through the crowd and clapped his old friend on the back.

"Hey man, you tryin' to get outta here without me?" Devin asked jokingly.

"Man, I thought I'd lost you," Ted replied, grabbing his friend and hugging him.

"This is the worst thing I've ever seen in my life," Ted continued between coughs.

"Yeah, pretty scary. I've seen some horrible things 'ya know in the past few hours. I'm not sure I'll ever forget," Devin confided.

"Yeah," Ted agreed looking off in the distance. He thought about the reflection he had seen of himself earlier. It made him sick. He would give anything just to get back to his office in San Francisco right now. He knew that things were going to start falling apart if he didn't act fast.

"Me too." he replied.

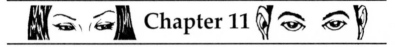 **Chapter 11**

Taylor and Camara sat at the petite breakfast nook table sipping Chai tea. The news was playing low on a small thirteen-inch television in the kitchen. All the news about the attack on the United States, The World Trade Centers and the Pentagon was being repeated every five minutes.

The most recent development had come in an hour ago. Apparently, a plane had also crashed somewhere in Pennsylvania. Although the numbers had been estimates, it was clear that the death toll would be significant.

Taylor sat her cup on the saucer and pushed it back, resting her arms on the edge of the table.

"I can't believe this," Taylor sighed. "How can this be happening? I could never imagine that I would be experiencing war in my lifetime, least of all fearing that my husband may be dead as a result of it."

"I know, I know. This is all so horrible," Camara agreed.

"And to top it off, it's been almost seven hours and people still can't get through most of the phone lines."

"It'll be okay. I'm sure Devin and Troy will be just fine...they have to be," Camara said biting her bottom lip.

"Oh I'm so sorry, Cam. I've been sitting here feeling sorry

for myself forgetting that you haven't heard from your brother either. He'll be okay. He's all you've got. They're all we've got," Taylor said moving to her friend's side of the table to comfort her. They sat there crying and rocking in each other's arms.

Troy had been like a little brother to Taylor too, often calling she and Camara for a female perspective when dealing with his girlfriends. At one time, before meeting Devin, Taylor had wished Troy were five years older. He was always wise beyond his years and incredibly responsive to the needs of women. Taylor knew he would find a woman who would cherish him and rightfully so, he was a good man.

As Taylor got up to reheat the water for their tea and get some more Kleenex, the phone rang. Both women froze and stared at one another. The phone rang a second time and Taylor haltingly made her way toward the wall phone.

"Hello."

"Hello, Mrs. Harris, this is the operator. I have a collect call from…"

It seemed as if an eternity had passed before the operator said the name. "Devin Harris, would-"

"Yes. Yes, I'll accept," Taylor screamed before the operator could finish her sentence.

"Is it him?" Camara asked running to her friend's side and placing her arm supportively around her shoulder.

"Yeah," Taylor managed, tears streaming down her face.

"I'll connect you now. Go ahead, sir."

"Devin, baby are you there? Are you okay?"

The line was filled with static, but she could hear his voice and it was the sweetest thing she had ever heard in her life.

"Taylor it's me. I'm fine. A little shaken but otherwise okay. How are you and the boys?"

"We're okay and missing you, of course!"

"Me too," Devin replied between static.

"Is that daddy?" The boys asked running into the kitchen and tugging at the phone.

"Wait a second, hold on baby, the boys want to say hi. Now very quickly boys, I don't know how much time the line will be clear."

"Hey dad," Jr. spoke as Chaz pulled at the phone.

Each of the boys spoke to their father as Taylor looked on. Tears continued streaming, unchecked down her cheeks.

"Okay boys, say goodbye," Taylor managed, removing the phone from her son's hand.

Devin Jr. and Chaz retreated reluctantly back to the family room to watch videos. Taylor refused to let them watch the unending news footage that played on every channel, but she also knew there were only so many videos they could watch before they too went stir crazy.

"Devin, honey when are you coming home? "

"I'm not sure. Every hour they announce that the airport will be opening soon, but it has yet to happen. But honey, I've seen some horrible things out here. I just thank God that we didn't make that meeting. People burning, people jumping out of buildings, people being trampled. And to see these huge, mammoth-like buildings reduced to rubble," Devin paused. "It's like nothing you could ever imagine."

The phone began to pop with static and fade in and out.

"Devin are you there?"

"I can barely hear you. I'll call you again when I get a chance. Love you."

The line went dead and Taylor clutched the phone as if holding it would bring Devin back.

"Is he gone?" Camara asked.

"Yeah, but he's okay. He's okay," Taylor said with relief.

"That's wonderful. I'm so happy for you."

The two women hugged fiercely wanting never to let go.

"I just know Troy will be okay too. Here, try his numbers again," Taylor said handing Camara the phone.

"I'm scared Taylor. I really don't have a good feeling about this."

"I know but you seen how the phone just gave out. The lines are not fully working yet. I'm sure he's probably trying to reach you."

Camara reluctantly dialed her brother's number for the eighth time and was greeted by the same response---all circuits are busy. She placed the phone back on its base and shook her head.

"I have no choice but to wait, for now. If I haven't heard from him by tonight, I'm taking the red-eye or the first flight I can to New York."

Taylor clutched her friend's trembling hand while they sat in silence.

"Ya know I have something that will help you." Taylor disappeared upstairs and returned with two small, oval-shaped pills.

"These will help you relax," Taylor said, placing the pills in Camara's hand.

"Taylor, these are Xanax...sleeping pills. I definitely don't want any."

"I don't mean for you to take them both now, just when you think you need it. And for you, maybe just one at a time."

Camara looked at her friend skeptically.

"Why do you have them?"

Taylor did not bother to go into the fact that her doctor would do virtually anything she asked of him. Taylor side-stepped the question and continued.

"This is really a mild dosage to help take the edge off."

"Take the edge off of what? Taylor, I'm really concerned about you having these at your disposal like this. I mean if you have trouble sleeping why not use a less severe way of getting to sleep. There are about a hundred different natural sleep aids; Chamomile, Hops, California Poppy, Catnip, Lemon Balm, Lavender, Skullcap and Valerian Root just to name a few."

"Camara, just hold on a minute! I have a very stressful job and a demanding lifestyle. You don't know what it's like to be me. I'm exhausted most of the time and then when I finally get a few hours to get some sleep; my mind is racing so fast that I can't. And today, I thought my husband had been killed because two planes ran into the building where he was to have a meeting. I mean for crying out loud, Camara. I need a break!"

Camara regarded her friend closely and then leaned in slightly so the boys would not overhear their conversation.

"Taylor, you know you've always been like a sister to me. I just want you to take care of yourself, that's all. This is not the way to solve any problem. We all have it hard. In fact, it will be a lot harder if you continue down this road."

Taylor nodded her head in agreement

"Does Devin know?" Camara asked.

"No. And after what he's been through, there's no way I… we can deal with this right now."

Taylor could tell her friend was concerned. They had always been on one accord. She honestly could not remember a single time when they had disagreed on anything. Had she really done anything so wrong? She just needed a little help to sleep. She was educated and smart with a coveted position in a large corporation. All she needed was a little time to pull things together. Once Devin returned, she felt things would be better…they had to be.

Taylor took the two pills as if she were washing them down the sink and quickly placed them under her tongue and dry-swallowed them. She quickly looked over her shoulder to make sure her friend had not seen.

There were six more pills that remained hidden in her nightstand. Once she finished them, that would be it for her.

Now more than ever, she needed to be able to get rest and relaxation. The world was changing right in front of her. She honestly wished she could take the rest of the pills and sleep until her pain just went away.

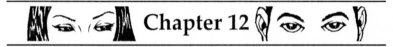 **Chapter 12**

Devin and Ted managed to catch one of the first flights out of LaGuardia after its re-opening. They arrived at San Francisco International Airport at 4:17 p.m. the next day. Devin had been nervous about boarding the plane after listening to all the news reports and conversations at the airport. Yet, his desire to get home and away from all he had witnessed in the past twenty-four hours was overpowering.

The tension on the plane was almost tangible. On a full flight, the quiet was eerie.

Ted sat typing away on his laptop as if they had been on just another business trip.

Devin was irritated by his friend's insensitivity to the situation. He was also irritated by the thoughts of his actions two nights ago that kept creeping into his mind.

He never intentionally set out to be unfaithful to Taylor. Things just seemed to happen. He had always had an insatiable appetite for sex, which for the most part had been satisfied when he and Taylor were dating. Eleven months into their marriage, the sex had never been better. Then, Taylor got pregnant. While they were both ecstatic about having a child, their social life suffered.

Anna Dennis

Taylor was sick from her first trimester right up to delivering Devin, Jr. It began with morning sickness and escalated to inability to sleep, mood swings, cravings, loss of appetite, false contractions, bleeding and ultimately mandatory bed rest that accompanied a strict no 'sexual intercourse' rule.

By that time it was a few weeks before her delivery date with the certainty of at least another four weeks before they could be intimate. However, there were other ways they could be intimate and it seemed as a good a time as any to explore the possibilities, but Taylor wanted no parts of it.

Soon, Devin began to take on the mood swings, irritability and loss of appetite. However, his member stayed hard as a rock. He thought he would never make it through that year, but he did. The following year and a half were almost like old times.

Then, she got pregnant with Charles and he knew he could not go through being deprived like that again.

One afternoon as Devin stood in line waiting to purchase a sandwich and head back to the office, he noticed an attractive woman walking across the street heading towards the sandwich shop where he stood. At first, he pretended not to notice her, but as she approached, it became more evident that she too had noticed him. She casually walked up to the line and stood behind him. He could smell the scent of her perfume. It was subtle, but it immediately aroused him. He turned to find her staring right at him.

"How are you today?" He asked.

"I'm fine and so are you," she said, smiling flirtatiously at him.

He was both embarrassed and excited by her forwardness.

"Why thank you." He replied. "I don't think I've seen you here before," Devin continued. "Do you work around here?"

"This is my third day working with a small venture

63

capital firm a couple of blocks from here."

Devin was even more intrigued. He and Ted had just started discussions about developing their own start-up venture. Maybe she could give him some insight. But then again, he tried not to mix business with pleasure.

"What do you do there?"

"I'm a Project Management Consultant. I go into organizations and help them develop a model for their business initiatives."

"Interesting."

"To some. I love the research and forecasting. Also, for new companies and departments, their excitement is contagious and for the moment, I become a part of the team."

"Except at the end of the day, you don't hate your boss," Devin joked. They both laughed as they moved up to the counter to order.

"Can I buy you lunch?" Devin offered smoothly, suddenly not wanting to rush back to the office.

"I'd like that very much."

Devin extracted a twenty-dollar bill from his wallet and paid for both sandwiches and a couple of ice teas. He followed her to a table for two in the rear of the delicatessen balancing their sandwiches and drinks on a tray. This gave him an opportunity to preview what was to come. He had already seen what she had to offer from the front. Pretty, honey complexion with full, nice-shaped lips and breasts. Her hair was cut into a trendy, layered style that rested comfortably on her shoulders. She looked as if she could have been Hispanic and Black or Puerto Rican. Devin liked what he seen from behind as well. She had a full bottom. Slightly larger than what he liked, but he was confident he could overlook that small imperfection. They sat down at the table. Devin wanted her bad, but he had to play it cool.

"I guess I should at least tell you my name."

"People who eat together usually do know at least that much." Devin chided.

"Melissa," she said extending her hand.

"Nice to meet you Melissa," Devin said taking her hand in his and holding it a little longer than necessary. He noticed there was no wedding ring, which was a plus. Although he had his on, that usually did not make one bit of difference with women like Melissa.

"I'm Devin."

"So what do you do?"

"I'm a bit of a consultant, too. A business partner and myself are considering developing a start-up."

"Really? Doing what?"

"This and that. It's really preliminary at this point." Devin said between bites of his sandwich, moving the conversation away from his personal life. He had not bought her lunch for conversation or an interview.

"That's great!"

"Yeah. So, when do you think I can see you again," Devin said looking at his watch. She smiled demurely and Devin knew he had to play this game direct and strategically. He knew her type. Educated, but a bit of a tease in the corporate world, because there was an image she had to uphold. But he would bet a nickel to a dollar that she had a completely different side to her behind closed doors.

"How about tonight?"

Cha Ching! "That'll work. How about 7:30?"

"Perfect."

"Why don't you write your number and address down here," Devin said, handing her a napkin. "And I'll see you then."

"Certainly. I can't wait." She said, scribbling her information on the napkin.

By 8:30 p.m. that evening, Devin and Melissa were on

round two and drenched in sweat. It had been just what Devin needed, rough, satisfying and emotionless sex.

As he sat on the plane watching his friend attempt to make a call from his cell phone, he shook his head. It was obvious that Ted did not feel well. He was coughing profusely and did not look quite himself. Maybe that was why he and Ted got along so well. Many people saw Ted as a pompous, arrogant, know-it-all. He saw Ted and saw a mirror image of himself. *Who am I to judge anyone?*, he thought ruefully.

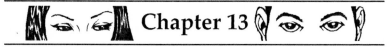 **Chapter 13**

Taylor sat in the window waiting for Devin. It had been the longest night of her life. Even with the sleeping pills, she did not get much more than two hours of sleep. Devin had been able to contact her from the plane to inform her of his time of arrival. He made her promise not to meet him at the airport because he had taken his car, but now Taylor wished she had not made that promise. He should be home by now, she thought.

Parking would be a mess with all the security that had been put in place since yesterday. She was going stir crazy just waiting since she had sent the boys off to school. Against their usual rule, she had allowed the boys to a school-night sleep over at the neighbors home. She reasoned that they needed a happy diversion in their lives right now. She agreed with psychologists that returning children back to their normal schedules as quickly as possible was essential in ensuring they would not be traumatized by this tragedy. She took another glance out the window. If the flight landed on time, he should have been pulling up to the house fifteen minutes ago. Her tea needed warming so she headed to the kitchen and turned the fire on low under the teapot.

Just as she was coming back from the kitchen, she heard

the garage door open. She froze. Then she heard the garage door closing. The sound of something so mundane and normal brought tears to her eyes.

She rushed through the door that connected the kitchen and garage. There, she saw a tired and weary-looking Devin, but he was home. He sat behind the steering wheel with his eyes closed.

Taylor hurried over to the driver's side of the car and opened the door.

"Devin," She whispered for fear that saying more would cause an onslaught of tears.

"Taylor, baby," Devin replied, hugging his wife. "You don't know how good it is to see you and to be home," he continued, still holding on to Taylor.

Taylor squeezed him in her arms and kissed his face, his neck, his forehead, his lips and he returned the favor. She wept openly and it felt good. Not only was she happy to see her husband and know that he was safe, but there had been so much going on in her life that she wanted to tell him and could not. All that seemed so insignificant now given what had happened in the last forty-eight hours.

"Baby don't cry. I'm all right," Devin assured her. "I'm home."

"I know," Taylor managed. "I just wish I could feel this way forever…close to you. I just love you so much. I don't know what I would've done if anything had happened to you."

Devin wiped away Taylor's tears with the pads of his thumbs. He kissed her on her forehead, her nose and then her lips where he lingered, teasing her tongue with his.

"I love you too," he whispered urgently as he continued planting kisses down her neck, coming to rest between her breasts. He carefully unbuttoned her white, low-cut blouse and unsnapped her bra. Taking one of Taylor's breasts in each of his hands, Devin gently suckled at the left and then the right one.

"Ooh, baby," Taylor moaned, pushing his head deeper into her cleavage. After a while, Devin lifted his head still massaging Taylor's breasts with his hands. They looked deep into each other's eyes, seeing the person each had fallen in love with many years ago. Mistakes and past sins forgiven, for the moment. They were young again. Life was pure and carefree and war was something you read about in history books.

"Where are the boys?" Devin asked between breaths.

"At the neighbors," Taylor managed.

Until now, Taylor had been sitting partially on the edge of the driver's seat and in Devin's lap. Devin unfastened his seat belt and then his trousers. He reclined the BMW's seat back as far as it would go and untied Taylor's wrap-around, denim skirt. It fell to the garage floor as did her panties. She climbed in on top of Devin and positioned herself atop his throbbing member.

Their bodies moved in perfect rhythm as they kissed, caressed and nurtured one another. Devin's slow, deliberate strokes made Taylor yearn for more. She gyrated her hips and clenched her thighs around Devin's manhood forcing him to move deeper and faster. Had their car not been a BMW, the vehicle's shocks would have been put to the test as the vehicle rocked back and forth. Taylor's breath caught in her throat and she braced both hands on Devin's seat. Devin's hands were everywhere, as if exploring his wife's body for the first time. He needed to feel safe and whole again and for the first time in a long time, he was making love to his wife and not just having sex. His release came and he yielded, mind and body to its ethereal affects. Somewhere in the distance, his mind whirled like a strong wind picking up force. Taylor joined him on his journey as her moans of ecstasy combined with the whistling teapot called to him like the light from a lighthouse beckoning ships in the distance.

Devin and Taylor lay in each other's arms. From the car, they had made their way upstairs to the bedroom where they explored one another further.

Devin traced small, languid circles on Taylor's stomach, while she smoothed the hair on his chest.

"I just don't think I could've dealt with it." Taylor said, breaking the silence. "I'm just so glad you got back home safely. It's just beyond my comprehension how anything this horrible could happen."

"Mine too. It's surreal. Honestly, I think I'm still in shock and probably will be for a long time. But of course, I'm one of the lucky ones. Taylor, the things I witnessed, no human being should ever have to see in their lifetime. Everybody in that area that survived will be scarred forever. People jumping out of windows one hundred or more stories up...it was horrific."

"I'm so sorry you had to be there." Taylor said, consoling her husband.

To see buildings as large as The World Trade Centers collapse in an incomprehensible cascade of steel and human lives was more than Devin could bear. The images put to shame those of World War II. In Devin's mind, September 11 had been one of the bloodiest days in the history of America.

"Oh, Devin! Where were you-What did you do?" Taylor continued.

"I honestly don't know what I did. I walked, I ran. I tried to help an elderly lady who had fallen. To know that both of those buildings are no longer there just boggles the mind."

"Baby, I know. It must have been a nightmare for you," Taylor said, rubbing the side of her husband's jaw.

"And the plane that was hijacked from Boston...it was so

scary. There were all sorts of rumors that one of the planes had been headed here for the Transamerica Building, just four buildings away from my office."

"This is all crazy! If anything happened to you and the boys, I couldn't take it."

"Me too, but we can't think like that. And what about the guys you had meetings with?" They both lay silent for a moment.

Devin's mind involuntarily went back to the night before, September 10th and he squeezed his eyes together to get rid of the image.

"We never met. Ted has been trying their office with no success. I'm sure it has been obliterated with everything else in those buildings. I guess we just wait and see with the rest of the world."

"Devin let's not even talk about this anymore. We're here now with each other and we're safe. Nothing's ever 'gonna come between us."

Taylor wished she believed what she was telling her husband. She remembered that a lot was riding on this trip to New York for them and their investors. It was going to take some time for things to get back on track, if they ever did. She was sure funding yet another start-up from California was not going to be on anyone's priority list.

There was no way she could go through footing the household bills again while Devin put another deal together. That would be too much pressure with the expenses they had. Things seemed to be like a roller coaster in the Harris household. One minute everything was blissful and the next minute you were holding on for dear life. It was anybody's guess what was going to happen next. Right now, she was thankful for the peace she had in the moment. She lay with her head buried in her husband's chest wishing she could make everything all right for the both of them.

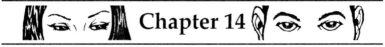

Chapter 14

Taylor rode the elevator up to the 38th floor of the forty-story building where her corner office was located. She was thankful for the Captivate screens that had been placed in the elevators four months earlier. They were the new trend in elevator television, replacing the dull elevator music that previously accompanied passengers on their ride.

Of course, since last week's horrible events the only news on Captivate was about New York's rescue efforts of those still believed buried in the rubble of the Twin Towers. The Dow had taken a nose-dive while shaken investors and wary consumers struggled with the fact that their country was at war and the uncertainty of yet another attack.

Taylor had taken the rest of the week off after Devin came home. She checked a few E-mail and voice mail messages, but otherwise decided staying home with her husband and comforting him was her prime objective. Oddly, the three days they spent together had been all the therapy they needed. It amazed her how from tragedy, something positive could be borne. They had reconnected physically, emotionally and spiritually and it had been unlike anything she had experienced since before they were married. She felt closer to him now more than ever and somehow the cloud of suspicion and deceit seemed to all but evaporate.

There was still the small issue of the Xanax that she had not shared with her husband. Even though they shared their feelings, it was more about Devin and his ordeal in New York than it was about her issues and she wanted to respect that. Also, it was a small enough issue that she felt she could take care of on her own. It was a cliché she had heard before, but she really could stop taking the pills anytime she wanted.

Taylor stepped off the elevator and walked through the lobby where the receptionist greeted her.

"Good morning Mrs. Harris how are you?" Trish asked flatly.

"Good morning Trish. I'm good. How are you?" Taylor asked. She noticed Trish seemed to be less enthusiastic than usual. Concern furrowed Taylor's brow. From the time she stepped out of her car and into the garage of her office building, she had to be on as VP of Human Resources. Her job, in addition to ensuring that the human resource laws and practices were being followed in the organization, was to show genuine concern. More often than not, she really could care less whether or not some spoiled director or other vice president received the raise they thought they should have. Or that they did not receive as many company shares or stocks as the next person. She had struggled without the help of anyone, not even, the then Vice President of Human Resources, to get where she was. Typically, the best part of her job was helping the struggling, secretaries, coordinators and managers fight for the raises or promotions they deserved.

She liked Trish. Her name was not shortened or abbreviated, simply Trish. Trish had been with the company for two years. She was very involved in the community and a die-hard environmentalist. Often times, Trish took the lead in coordinat

-ing many of the volunteer activities and team-building events for the executive floors. Her infectious smile and outgoing personality was why Taylor had hired her. To see her acting differently was of concern to Taylor.

"I'm okay I guess. This whole 9/11 disaster has me really upset. I just feel weirded out now...like I need to do something."

"Why don't we talk about it? Come with me into my office." Taylor knew she had back-to-back meetings starting in the next half-hour, but she would rather handle this issue now rather than later.

"I feel badly about bending your ear like this on your first day back in the office. You haven't even had your latte? yet."

"Don't worry about it", Taylor said, closing the door behind them and laughing.

"I'll need more than caffeine before today is over."

She switched on her computer and removed several documents from her briefcase. Trish had taken a seat at the mini conference table in Taylor's office.

Taylor quickly scanned through twelve voice mail messages to see if there was anything urgent. Fortunately, there was not. She then joined Trish at the conference table with her notepad and pen in hand.

"So, what's on your mind?"

"Well, 'ya know how I'm really involved with saving our environment, specifically the Rain Forest, right?"

"Yes, okay."

"Well, since last week, I just feel like what I'm doing here is not utilizing me for anything that makes an impact to the environment."

Taylor gauged her response carefully. The truth was that unless you hired a senior citizen looking to make some additional money while in retirement, the most you could expect from a good receptionist was two years, three years tops. If they had any aspirations at all, they would want to move on to something more challenging.

"Well Trish, you will have been here two years next month. Maybe it is time for something different. You're excellent at coordinating the department volunteer projects. Maybe you can run a program through our Community Relations department that deals specifically with environmental issues. Maybe it's a recycling program or getting the company involved in Spare The Air Day."

"Mrs. Harris, those sound good for starters, but eventually, I mean something really significant like leading a protest and forming a committee that challenges government policy on war and weapons."

"I see. Well, that's a very political move Trish and the last time I checked, it didn't pay very well."

Both women laughed. "I don't mean to make light of your beliefs or offend you," Taylor offered apologetically.

"No offense taken, but...I mean is bombing going to make us safer? It's so unnecessary. "

"The insidious feature of terrorism is that the guys who did this are dead, except Osama Bin Laden," Taylor said shaking her head.

"I don't know if the way to honor the dead is by killing more innocent people. I'm just sick about this whole thing and yet it has brought into focus for me...what is the next step after receptionist...administrative assistant, secretary? I just don't want to deal with the politics of it all."

Taylor nodded her head in agreement, reflecting on her own journey to get where she was now. Sadly, Trish would probably have an easier time getting a vice president position than she had and she didn't even have a degree yet and at her current course, apparently had no interest in obtaining one.

The truth was, she had no idea how politics would come

into play if she pursued a career in the corporate world. Taylor could understand where she was coming from.

"Trish how would you like for me to help you? Do you feel like you need time off?"

"I don't know Mrs. Harris. Honestly, I'm confused. I just need time to think. I feel depressed about everything and at this point a little scared."

Taylor could identify with Trish more than she could admit to herself.

"Tell you what...why don't you take a week off and see how you feel. I'm no psychiatrist, but I think you're suffering from post-traumatic stress syndrome or something. I'm sure a lot of people are. You do know as part of our company's insurance benefits, we have psychiatrists our employees can talk to. We'll just get a temp and play it by ear."

"Trish looked relieved. "I think I'd like that," she smiled.

Taylor patted her shoulder reassuringly. Her phone buzzed and before she could answer it, there was a quick knock on the door before it opened. Taylor expected that it would be her secretary, but it was her boss, Jim McNeeley.

"Taylor, I need a minute as soon as you're done." Mr. McNeeley said. Taylor was not scheduled to meet with him until later this afternoon. What was so important that he needed to interrupt her...something he never did. Taylor's mouth went dry.

"I'm finished up here Jim. We can meet now. Trish, think about what I said and we can talk at the end of the day."

Trish nodded in Taylor's direction, gathered her belongings and quickly left the office. Mr. McNeeley closed the door behind her and took a seat on the opposite side of Taylor's desk, facing her.

"How are you doing after last week?" Mr. McNeeley asked getting comfortable in his chair. "You been feeling okay?"

he continued.

"Pretty good. I think it was the best thing for me to be with my family. Particularly, my husband, with him being so close to it and all."

"Yes. I can't imagine what both of you must've gone through on that day. That was a terrible day for everyone."

Taylor tried to make direct eye contact with her boss to see where he was going with this conversation. She had left him a voicemail message on Wednesday explaining to him that she was going to be out for the rest of the week and providing him with a brief outline as to why. On Tuesday, September 11th, she learned from Trish that executive staff members were telling people to go home as they arrived in the lobby of the building...few that there were. The office was closing, so it made no sense for her to come all the way in for nothing.

Mr. McNeeley kept his eyes trained on the partial view of the Bay Bridge that could be seen from the picture window in Taylor's office.

"Yeah, that morning employees really looked to the executives in Human Resources to provide direction. Many did not know whether to come in or not. They were conflicted, just like everyone else. You see Taylor part of being a Vice President of Human Resources is being a leader...even in times of crisis. Frankly, I'm concerned about you. You've seemed edgy and just a little distracted lately."

Taylor could feel the blood rush to her head and immediately, she felt a headache beginning at the base of her skull and working its way to her right temple. The only thing she wanted more desperately than two Excedrin right now was to curse him out so badly that it made his mother cry. Instead, she sat there, nodding politely at the appropriate times and fighting to look relaxed and reassured when every nerve ending was ablaze.

At some point, she tuned him out and tried to think pure,

peaceful thoughts. Devin Jr. and Chaz came to mind. A vivid image of her kissing their feet when they were babies flashed in her mind. She could hear them laughing and giggling. The room was silent and Taylor surmised that he must be done with his lecture.

"Well Jim, there's been a lot going on the past week or so."

"I understand that, but my concern began well before September 11. I just felt this was a good time to tell you. This tragedy has caused people to really reflect on their past and future. Myself included. Might not hurt for you to get things back on track...back into perspective 'ya know?"

Taylor could feel her insides churning. She needed some air.

"...So just take this time to get things back on track, Taylor. You're still pretty new at this, but showing exemplary leadership is the stuff greats are made of. Don't get me wrong," he rambled. "I totally understand and sympathize with your family situation. Particularly thinking you'd lost your husband, but this is just advice going forward. Your position comes with a lot of responsibility."

He looked Taylor directly in the eyes for the first time since he had entered her office. Taylor could tell he was searching for her reaction, but she was determined not to give him the satisfaction.

"I was going to wait to have this conversation with you on Friday, but I thought it'd be best to get it out of the way."

Once Taylor was sure he had finished, she put on her best Colgate smile.

"Jim, thank you. I really appreciate your concern and your advice. I'll make a concerted effort to demonstrate more leadership and initiative in the future. By the way, are we still on for our 3:00 o'clock this afternoon?"

Jim was taken aback. "Uh sure, I think so." He pulled out

his Palm Pilot as though he needed to verify that the 3:00 o'clock meeting was actually on his schedule. "Yeah, that will be fine. I guess I'll see you again at three."

"Looking forward to it," she lied.

With that, he opened the door and disappeared down the hall. Taylor was dumbfounded. She could not believe what she had just heard. With her head pounding, she managed to get to the door and close it. She plopped back down in her chair with her hands shaking so badly she could hardly hold her pen. The absolute nerve of him to insinuate that she had somehow failed in her job responsibilities, was insulting. He was making close to $300,000 a year and she could not point to one thing he had done since he'd been at the company. Other than brown-nose the CEO and COO; he was virtually good for nothing.

One time after a grueling half-day meeting, an executive had joked that Jim had his nose so far up the CEO's butt, he could probably smell what he had eaten for lunch. She could not have agreed more.

Taylor was sure he would use this as an excuse to chip away at her end-of-the-year bonus. Just who did he think he was talking to? To tell her that she should be at her post rather than with her family was ridiculous. Why did people always feel they had to have control over everything just because you worked for them? Rather than him concerning himself with making sure the organization was exercising its human resources policies and practices with the employees, he was too busy watching her.

Suddenly she felt the need to get out of her office before she screamed. She minimized the document on her computer screen, retrieved her purse from the side drawer of her desk and left her office.

Taylor stopped by her secretary, Karen's desk, but she was not there. She then stopped by Trish's area and waited for her to finish her call.

"Trish, I've left a note for Karen, asking that she clear my calendar, but if anyone asks, I'll be telecommuting for the rest of the day."

"Okay." Trish responded.

Taylor turned on her heels and headed toward the bank of elevators. She needed to get to the pharmacy quickly to refill her prescription. No one seemed to understand what she was going through, not even her best friend. Everyone thought Taylor was invincible. But soon it would not matter...sweet relief was coming.

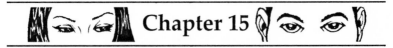 **Chapter 15**

Ted sat in the doctor's examining room waiting to be seen. He hated visiting any medical facility. There was never anything good that came of the visits. He always waited until there were no other options before seeing the doctor.

Absently fingering the purple lesion on his forearm, he thought about his loss of energy and appetite. The cough he had was now into its second month. Neither his appetite for sex nor his ability to perform had been hampered to date, but he feared that above all else. With his recent difficulty breathing after one of his coughing attacks, he was at a loss as to what was going on with his body.

There was a light tap on the door and then a doctor appeared.

"Mr. Levingston," the doctor murmured more to himself than to Ted. "I'm Dr. Whittier," he said reviewing Ted's chart. "What seems to be the problem?" he asked looking at Ted for the first time.

Dr. Whittier was a fifty-something year old man, about five foot seven inches tall with dark brown hair that had just begun to gray at the temples. His glasses made him look older and more knowledgeable. Ted began to feel at ease.

"Well, I've just been really tired lately, more so than ever. And, I've had this cough that I can't seem to get rid of. All the over-the-counter stuff doesn't work, so I'm hoping to get some cough syrup with codeine or something."

"Let's see what's going on here," Dr. Whittier said removing his stethoscope from around his neck. "You know, you were supposed to remove your shirt and put on the gown," Dr. Whittier joked. "It's hard to find good patients these days."

"I know, I'm just not used to this. I've always been as healthy as a horse." Ted responded while removing his shirt.

Dr. Whittier listened intently. He asked Ted to breathe in and out. He then checked his eyes, ears, nose and throat.

"So, you say this cough has been going on for about a month now?"

"Yeah, give or take a week." Ted replied nervously.

Dr. Whittier concluded his examination by checking Ted's thyroid glands and lymph nodes. "Well Mr. Levingston, it would appear that you have pneumonia. Your lungs are filled with fluid and that concerns me with someone of your age."

"Pneumonia?" Ted asked emphatically.

"Yes. Now, I need to ask you a couple of questions. Have you had diarrhea or fever during the time you've had this cough?"

Ted had to think long and hard. He was still trying to get his mind around the fact that he had pneumonia.

"So is this like what some people call 'walking pneumonia'?"

"Absolutely. You've been totally functional, yet sick. So have you exhibited any of these other symptoms?"

"Yeah, I had diarrhea a couple of weeks ago, but it was right after September 11. I was in New York when the Towers were attacked so I just chalked it up to nerves. And because it went away, I didn't think anything of it."

"Okay Mr. Levingston. This is what I want to do. I'm going to prescribe an antibiotic to clear up the fluid in your lungs, but I also want you to go to the lab and have some blood work completed right away."

"What's the rush? Is there something else going on?"

"I'm not sure, but the labs will help me determine if there is, so the sooner I get the results back, the sooner I have a clear picture on everything."

Dr. Whittier wrote out the prescription and a lab work form. He handed the form to Ted, wrote some notes in his file and then placed his pen back in the pocket of his lab coat.

"I need to see you back in two weeks so I can take a listen to your lungs and go over the results of your blood work with you okay?"

"Okay," Ted replied, feeling as if he had been kicked in the stomach.

Dr. Whittier turned and left, leaving Ted feeling more alone than he could ever remember.

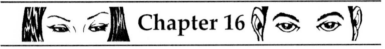 **Chapter 16**

Taylor and Camara drove in silence save for the horns that could be heard on the busy New York City streets. The cab driver maneuvered expertly through upper Manhattan, using his horn here and there to communicate to the other drivers. On a trip to New York about ten years ago with Devin, Taylor found it hard to believe that people drove and communicated that way. By the end of their trip, she came to understand and appreciate it. It was almost as if each honk of the horn represented a word or phrase, one honk: go, two honks: getting over and so on. She wished California drivers could be as sophisticated.

They were on their way to the airport after spending three days in New York. This was definitely not a girl's get-a-way as they had taken on several occasions. Had it not been for the grim circumstances, Taylor could count on her friend's quick wit and upbeat attitude. It hurt her to see her friend in this type of pain. It was her turn to be strong for her friend and for herself.

Unfortunately, Camara's brother, Troy, had been killed as a result of the World Trade Center attacks. Camara shook her head.

"You know, it's ironic that Troy was one of the lucky

ones…his body was actually found because he was not in either of the Towers, just near them. Hit by falling debris and crushed to death…funny how anything about that could seem lucky, but so many are still missing."

Troy had been a very handsome, thirty-two year old Information Technology Director for a software engineering firm.

"It's a horrible situation Cam," Taylor said soothingly as she held her friend.

"His entire life was ahead of him. He was on the fast track with a successful career ahead of him, a beautiful fiancée and unbeknownst to him, a baby on the way. A baby he will never have the opportunity to love or cradle in his arms."

"I know, but you can't dwell on that Cam…it only makes it worst. He left someone behind for you to love…his child. And that baby will always be a reminder, a part of Troy to let you know that he is still here."

"Thank you," Camara responded, choking back tears.

"For what?"

"For being my friend."

His funeral had been a closed casket service. Yet it was a tribute and a testament to the type of life he led; private and low-key. The small church in Midtown had been overflowing with family, friends, co-workers and even people from the local gym where he worked out. New York and the country had pulled together and become a family from this tragedy. It seemed the city had a funeral or memorial everyday they were there. And the entire city, it seemed, made every effort to attend.

Camara had finally made it to the point where she could go ten to fifteen minutes at a time without crying. She and Troy had shared the same bond twins share even though they were five years apart.

"You 'gonna be okay?" Taylor asked, grabbing her friend's hand and holding it.

"Yeah, someday. But I can tell you it's not going to be anytime soon. I mean why do horrible things have to happen to good people? You've got gang members, child molesters, people who have committed unspeakable acts of violence and of all those people, this tragedy has to hit and kill off so many good, hard-working people who had children and families. I just don't understand." Camara had begun to cry again.

Taylor could not think of one thing to say that would comfort her friend. She knew that if it had been Devin's funeral they were coming from, they would have to have carried her out on a gurney.

"In time Cammie, it will be all right. I can't explain why bad things happen to good people. All I know is that there is a reason and only God knows it."

"I'm sure he does Taylor, but I really wish he could tell me why all the people I love keep being taken away from me. Am I such a horrible person? What did I do to deserve having my husband taken by another woman and my brother taken by a bunch of psychotic foreigners who hate America?"

"Look Camara, torturing yourself this way is not going to do anyone any good. Remember when you first laid eyes on John? You thought he was the finest specimen of a man that ever walked the earth."

"What's your point?"

"Well, I disagreed," Taylor said jokingly. "But my point is that people are placed in our lives and taken from our lives for a reason. Sometimes it's for a short stay and other times it's longer. The bottom line is that we can't start blaming ourselves and stop living because we too were put here for someone. I'm still here for you and you for me. I don't know why Troy is gone, but in time, the pain won't hurt as much...I promise."

"You're right, Taye. But, he didn't deserve this. I just wish I knew why. He didn't deserve this at all," Camara said crying uncontrollably.

Taylor could only rock back and forth while hugging her friend. The truth was that she shared some of the same questions Camara had. She didn't know why bad things happened to good people. And she didn't know why bad people got away with doing bad things, but then again just like every other human; there was a lot she didn't know. If you sat pondering the meaning of life, you would be far more confused than when you started.

Camara had composed herself once again. She turned to Taylor, wiping at her eyes and dabbing her nose.

"Taylor?"

"Yes."

"Are you still taking those pills?"

Taylor was caught off guard.

"Promise me something, will you?" Camara asked.

"Absolutely."

"Stop the pills. I don't want to lose you too."

"Camara, I--"

"Taylor we've been best friends for a long time. I really need you to promise me this one thing. We've never lied to each other before. No excuses, no lies. Promise me."

Taylor listened to the urgency in her friend's voice and the desperation in her eyes. Camara was like a sister to her and there was not much she wouldn't do for her. The truth was, she never wanted to get addicted to Xanax. She just wanted the pain to go away. She wanted some solace from the chaos that was her life. Somewhere in the process, she became selfish and didn't care how the outcome might affect those she loved and who loved her.

Devin coming home safely and Troy being killed were two prime examples that you could not run and hide in your private little cocoon and not deal with life. Situations were going to arise, that was life. But ultimately, it was how you dealt with them that defined your moral fiber and character.

Maybe from Devin's close call and Troy's untimely and unexpected demise, her lesson was to appreciate life to the fullest. She also had two wonderful sons that she needed to be around for.

"Yes, I promise," Taylor replied, praying that she would be able to keep her promise to herself and to her friend.

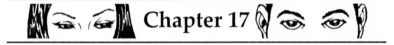 **Chapter 17**

Devin sat at his computer running figures for the company. The Dow was down and investors were in a panic selling everything and clutching tight to their purse strings. He let out a sigh amazed at how every time he decided to jump into something it went south. His savings were fine for now, but if he continued to sink money into a business that wasn't making any and supporting his personal expenditures, he would be broke in no time.

This was a very trying time. Peter and Craig were assumed dead, along with everyone else in the firm, except for one secretary who was running late on September 11 because her son had been ill that morning. The investment firm had been obliterated and yet, if Ted had not forgotten his Palm Pilot that morning they too would have been two more casualties of that fateful day. One week they're having conversations every day with this firm and its partners and the next none of it exists anymore.

It had been three months, but it still seemed like yesterday. Devin was not sure that even with all the time that had elapsed, it had really sunk in. He almost died. The country was at war. Why had his life been spared when so many others had perished? People he knew. It was scary, bizarre, real and very surreal all at the same time.

He was thankful for his two sons and had been making a concerted effort to spend as much time with them as possible. Football and basketball games had become routine for him in addition to helping with homework. It was a nice change of pace that allowed Taylor to have a break. Every Monday, he cooked dinner since he wasn't putting in twelve and fourteen hour days anymore. Their firm was still busy, but now the focus was different. Ninety percent of their time was spent seeking investors and the other ten percent was spent developing their model and its surrounding infrastructure.

Somehow he and Taylor's marriage seemed to be stronger since he came back from New York. He knew he had been changed; there was no question about that. But somehow, he believed Taylor too had been changed by the events of that fateful day. They had been through their share of ups and downs always returning to their same reclusive selves, unable to agree on anything. No amount of counseling or vacationing had done either of them any good.

Often times it took loss or near loss to make you appreciate what you had. He had taken his wife and children for granted far too long. It was always the assumption that things would remain the same and they would be there for him whenever he was ready. Being in New York on September 11 forced him to re-evaluate his thinking.

He typed in the ticker symbol for a local competitor to see how their stock was faring. He winced. Maybe things could be worse. In any event, he and Ted needed to have a meeting. Glancing at his watch he noted that it was already lunchtime. He stretched and headed for the door. Maybe he could coerce Ted to have a quick lunch and they could discuss their upcoming meeting with new investors. He grabbed his suit jacket and headed for Ted's office about thirty steps away. The door was ajar but to Devin's surprise it was quiet. Usually Ted would have on his headset, talking one hundred miles a minute as he gazed out the window upon the expansive view.

Devin tapped lightly on the door and pushed it open. Ted quickly shoved some papers in his desk.

"Hey man, what's up?" Devin asked.

"Oh you know, just tryin' to hustle something up here," Ted replied nervously.

"Yeah, well what are you workin' on?" Devin continued to pry, trying to figure out why Ted was acting so weird. He had never seen this man lose his cool or his resolve in all the years they had been friends. Something was very wrong and it would take some doing to try and finesse it out of him. However, if it had to do with the company, he trusted that Ted would readily share that information. After all, they were equal partners in this business.

"Oh the usual, just trying to rustle us up some investors and figure out what's next." Ted's voice trailed off for a minute. He re-focused, closed his drawer and shuffled some papers on his desk.

"Yeah, well why don't we take a break and go grab a bite to eat. I got a couple things I want to run by you."

"I got a lot of paperwork I need to finish up here. You know it's crazy right now."

"I can appreciate that, but you need to eat and since when have I needed to twist your arm to grab a bite with me?"

Ted pushed back from his desk and threw up his hands in mock defense. "Okay, okay. Let's go. I was always the sales-man, but I could never win an argument with you."

"Well I wish you could convince Taylor of that. I'm bat-ting zero after all these years."

"Humph, after all these years, to have somebody by your

side when times get rough, that's worth losing an argument here and there," Ted said reaching for his jacket hanging on the back of the door.

"Since when did you become the poster child for marriage and monogamy?"

"You know a lot of things have changed since we were in New York. I have changed since we were there. You told me that you changed. I think everybody has as a result of that day."

The two men left Ted's office and boarded the elevator. The five other people on the elevator caused Ted to halt his conversation. Fortunately, there was only one stop before reaching the lobby.

"So you were saying," Devin urged.

"Nothing really, just rambling. So what did you want to talk to me about?"

"Initially I wanted to talk about what our plans are for pitching to investors in this slowing economy, but I think that can wait. What's up with you man? You don't seem to be yourself."

Devin and Ted walked into the nearby Chinese food restaurant where they took a seat at a back table. Ted was thankful that his appetite had somewhat returned to normal. Maybe he could somehow get through this lunch without having to tell Devin what was really going on. Although Devin was like a brother to him, he was not ready to reveal his horrible secret to anyone. He was not even sure how he was going to deal with it himself. Somehow, admitting it to someone else would make it real. He was just not ready for that. A forty-ish, Asian waitress appeared with her tablet in hand.

"What you order?" she asked.

Both Devin and Ted has been to this restaurant so often that they did not need to look at the menus.

"We'll have a platter of fried rice, beef and broccoli and

lemon chicken," Devin replied, ordering for both of them. Once the waitress left, he directed his focus back to Ted.

"So, what gives?" Devin asked again.

Within minutes the waitress appeared with the platter of steaming fried rice. Devin immediately began heaping spoonfuls onto his plate. Another waitress delivered the beef and broccoli and lemon chicken.

"Oh, well you know. I'm going through it with one my lady friends. That's all," Ted replied feeling sick to his stomach at the sight of all the food.

Devin gathered a pile of the steaming fried rice onto his chopsticks, placed it in his mouth and began chewing. "Now I know something is wrong," he said between bites. "Once a player always a player. I can't believe you've let one get to you."

"No, nothing as drastic as all that," Ted replied picking at his rice.

Devin put down his chopsticks and looked Ted square in the eye. "Look man, what gives?" he asked, with an edge to his voice that caused people at the nearby table to stare. "Are you going to quit playing games and tell me what's going on or not? You're acting crazy and not eating. I know it's tough right now but if something else is going on, I need to know, now!"

Ted sat perfectly still. He wanted to tell his friend what was going on but he needed more time to digest his own dilemma. He pushed his chair back fed up with the inquisition.

"I can't have this conversation right now, man."

"What? Have you lost your mind?"

"Yeah, I have."

Ted walked out of the restaurant and to the parking garage. He had not done anything productive all morning; hopefully he could change that now. There were people he needed to contact and for once, money or sex was not his motivation.

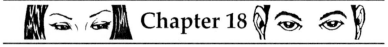 Chapter 18

Devin paced back and forth in his bedroom. It seemed these days he didn't know whether he was coming or going. Every time he recovered from one thing there was something else to deal with. He stood at the open window and allowed himself to bask in the warm sun. A cool breeze blew in from the coast reminding him of how much he used to enjoy this view.

Many times he would look out this very same window and gaze upon his handiwork in the backyard. Once there had been various, beautiful rose bushes growing. Splashes of white, pink, yellow and red bloomed every week. The fragrant aroma often found its way up to their bedroom window. His lawn used to be perfectly manicured. That seemed so long ago.

Now, some landscaper named Javier came once a week and did a lackluster job at best. There were brown patches of grass here and there and two of the four rose bushes were near dead.

Devin sighed. Somewhere in his quest for money, he had gotten away from the basics and now everything was falling apart. The call a few minutes ago from the local pharmacy had rattled him.

Normally, he would not even be at home this early, but

there was very little going on at the office and for once he felt more productive at home. Ted still had not given any specifics on what was wrong and why he stormed out of the restaurant a couple of weeks ago. At least he was acting more normal these days. Because Devin did most of the bookkeeping, he could not see where any monies or funds were being misappropriated.

Today was a new and even more confusing day. He learned from a telephone call that his wife needed to refill her prescription of Xanax. This, needles to say, concerned him. Had he been that out of touch? Surely there had to have been some outward signs exhibited. Yet, he had missed them all.

Chaz and Devin, Jr. bounded up the stairs and into the hallway, breaking into Devin's meandering thoughts. He walked briskly to the bedroom doorway and caught his sons in the act of play wrestling. DJ had his younger brother in a head-lock.

"Okay you two. What are your mom and I always telling you about running in the house and wrestling?"

"Mom always yells for us to stop or else. I can't remember what you tell us daddy." Chaz replied.

Devin felt as if the wind had been knocked out of him. It had been confirmed. He might as well have been living in another country for the past few years. They all seemed to be virtual strangers living under the same roof.

"You're stupid," Devin Jr. replied. "Dad always told us to stop running in the house or stop wrestling each other or else he'd get his belt."

"First of all don't call your brother stupid. Second, that is correct. So no more of those wrestling moves." Devin put on the best stern face he could muster and then tousled each of the boys' hair.

"Now get washed up so we can put burgers on the grill."

"Yippee," Chaz squealed with delight as they ran down

the hall.

Devin heard the front door open. He shook his head, knowing that he should wait until after the boys were in bed, but unable to restrain his desire to get to the bottom of this.

After a few minutes he heard Taylor stop in the boy's room and greet them with kisses and hugs. *It all seems so normal,* he thought. Soon, she appeared in their bedroom, briefcase in hand. She walked over to Devin who was now sitting in a chair in the retreat area of the their room.

"Hi honey," she said and kissed Devin affectionately on the lips.

"Hey," he responded, not looking directly at her nor returning her kiss.

Immediately, Taylor knew something was wrong, but she was not about to broach whatever the subject may be.

"How was your day today? Mine was non-stop all day." Taylor rambled on hoping Devin would put off whatever had him upset.

"Taylor, let's not play games here. I was home when the pharmacy called about your refill prescription of Xanax. Now, I don't know why you ever started taking them, but I'm definitely at a loss as to why you're having them refilled like vitamins or something!"

Taylor's mouth went dry. She had never gotten around to telling him about her little problem. It seemed there was always so much going on. It had been almost a month since she had taken them. Sure, a few Excedrin P.M. here and there had helped her along the way, but she also did not see taking something to help you sleep as a problem.

Unfortunately, she had an arrangement with her doctor to just have them refilled automatically. Had she still been taking them, the pharmacy would never have had the opportunity to call because she would have been there when their doors opened to pick up the prescription.

"Devin...I don't take them anymore. I haven't for a while."

"How long is a while?"

"Almost a month."

"That's not that long and why were you on them in the first place?"

"Because I had trouble getting to sleep."

"Trouble sleeping? You're always telling me how tired you are," Devin replied, his voice raising an octave.

"It's not the same. I was tired...am tired, exhausted even. But, there was so much on my mind that I still couldn't sleep."

"Help me to understand, Taylor. 'Cause I just don't get it. I mean are you or were you hooked on these things?"

"I wouldn't say that."

"Well, what would you say?"

Taylor could understand Devin being upset but she was not about to go through his interrogation after working a ten-hour day.

"I would say we need to have this conversation later," she said heading to their walk-in closet and removing her shoes.

"Oh, I guess you figure you've lied to me all this time, what's a few more hours, huh?"

"Devin grow up! Weren't you about to start dinner? I'll help. I mean we should have this discussion later."

"So I learn that my wife is a dope fiend and I'm suppose to hold my tongue about it?"

Taylor blew out an exasperated breath. She had had enough. With all the stuff she had put up with over the years, she was not about to be talked to like she was crazy.

"Dope fiend? Look," Taylor began, as she removed her suit jacket and earrings as if squaring off for a physical altercation. "Last time I checked, I was a grown woman. In the history of our marriage I don't ever recall having to get your permission for anything. Whatever I tell you is a courtesy and out of respect for our marriage. You are blowing this way out of proportion!"

"You think?" Devin retorted.

"Yes I do. Now let me stay out all night with one of my friends that we both know is nothing more than a whore and pretend we had a business meeting. Then you've got reason to get up in my face. But until that happens don't treat me like I'm some type of starry-eyed teenager who doesn't know her right from her left."

"You know," Devin began, rising from his chair. "That is so typical of you to take the attention off of your screw ups and turn the tables."

"I don't believe you! It's also typical of you to play dumb when the topic of your screwing around comes up."

"What are you talking about?"

"You have a very convenient and selective memory. Let me help you out. Let's see, Tamara, Shar, Lynn, Stephanie and let's not forget your little Geisha, Miko, just to name a few.

"I'm not going to have this conversation with you, Taylor."

"Oh I see, now you don't want to talk. Well that's really convenient, but not surprising. Do you think I'm stupid? You screw around under the guise of doing business and you wonder why I've got so much on my mind that I can't sleep?" Taylor managed with tears in her eyes. "I'm tired of having to be strong. I'm just so tired of it all," she sobbed.

Devin stood dumbfounded wondering what had just happened. He didn't know where to start. He knew Taylor suspected he had been unfaithful, but he had no idea that she had actual names. He wondered how much more she knew. Yet to engage her in this conversation was like walking into a land mine. The truth was, he could not admit to anything because to do so would make it more real for both of them and the damage would be irreparable. He was not prepared to lose his family over some women that meant absolutely nothing to him.

He walked over to Taylor and put his arms around her and held her tight. They stood in the middle of their bedroom holding one another while Taylor purged herself of the stresses and pain of life. Taylor felt safe in Devin's embrace. Nothing else in the world mattered right now.

They stood for a long while in that position, reconnecting mentally and spiritually without words. At one point Devin Jr. quietly approached and stood in the doorway, observing his mom and dad.

"Is mom okay?" he asked.

"She's fine. You and your brother go and watch TV and we'll be down in a few," Devin responded.

"Okay." Devin Jr. reluctantly left the doorway and headed down the hall.

"Taylor?" Devin spoke when they were alone again. "Are you okay?"

"Yeah," she replied, though her head remained nestled in the strong, chiseled comfort of Devin's chest.

"I'm so sorry, baby. I know how hard it must be for you. I'm sure it always has been. You're right, I always expect for you to be strong, no matter what and it never occurred to me that you might be tired. Whatever you're going through, we'll get through it, together."

Taylor looked up and gave just a hint of a smile but did not respond.

"Taylor I love you and only you. I always have."

"I know you love me Devin, but I'm not sure if you respect me." Taylor said, loosening their embrace and looking her husband in the eye. "Love means different things to different people. But I think for everyone it encompasses faithfulness

100

and respect."

"Taylor of course I respect you."

"How do you respect me if you're sleeping with other women?"

Devin released their embrace and sat on the edge of the bed. He did not want to have this conversation, but it appeared that if he wanted to make peace, there was no way around it.

"Taylor I'm not sleeping with other women. I'm not sleeping with anyone but you. All the women you mentioned, I have not slept with them. Yes, Ted and I may have been in the company of some of them, but I explained to you years ago what some of these settings are like when we meet with potential investors."

"Yeah," Taylor sighed thoughtfully. "You know some people would probably call me a fool for believing you every time. But the heart is really something. They say it's the strongest muscle in our body, but I guess it's the weakest muscle in mine because I love you no matter what. Part of me wants to track you down no matter where you go and find out the truth...I mean really see it for myself. Sadly, I don't think my seeing it would even make a difference. The other part of me doesn't want to know anything. I've had to live years with that inner battle and conflict. That's where the sleeping pills came into play. I just needed to get away from thinking and give my mind a rest. That's all."

It was Devin's turn to tear up now. He had been touched by his wife's admission. She had bared her soul and that really made him love her and trust her more. He was saddened that he could not be as honest. It would destroy lives. Not only theirs, but their sons as well. Despite her forgiving nature, to admit his indiscretions to her would be something she could never get past. But he was telling the truth when he said he loved her. Without question he did and he was sure he would never love any woman as much.

"Taylor, I understand. I really do. We've both got a lot of healing we need to do…together."

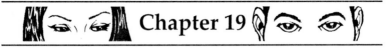 **Chapter 19**

Ted lay in bed staring at the ceiling. He glanced at the digital display clock on his nightstand. It was 2:43 a.m. This was becoming the norm. He would go to bed at 10:00 or 11:00 p.m., toss and turn and then be fully awake by 2:30 or 3:00 a.m. It never occurred to him the type of things one thought about when they had hours of down time. Sleeplessness was never something he suffered from, nor was sleeping alone. Not since his early college days had he ever had more than seven days pass where there was not someone to share his bed with. He had gotten accustomed to being lonely but never being alone. But life had a funny way of catching up with you.

Although he had a lot on his mind, namely his mortality, that was not his immediate concern. What he wanted now and had wanted for the past several weeks as morbid as the thought was, was sex. He laughed to himself. He was conflicted.

Maybe if he had been one of the nerds in college his life would be different...a wife, two or three kids a house. But who was he kidding? That might have lasted a minute before he became bored out of his mind. Variety was the spice of life and he believed in having plenty of variety.

Unfortunately, that was why his life was in such turmoil

now. Who could have imagined that an act that gave so much pleasure could cause so much pain? His life would be different from now on and yet he too had changed the course of several peoples lives since the day he learned he was HIV positive over a month ago. There was no way he could tell someone he was HIV and expect them to still want to have sex with him. Of course, Magic Johnson had told the world he was HIV positive, but he was married and therefore, still having plenty of protected sex, but sex nonetheless.

Ted had a problem rationalizing the notion of HIV and AIDS. Everyone knew basketball players had women in every city where their games were scheduled so the question of Magic's sexual preference never really came into play. People still looked at the average person with HIV and questioned whether they were homosexual or partook in intravenous drug use. There was a curiosity to know how it was contracted so the person could immediately be labeled. Although he was neither gay nor did he use drugs, he could not live with people having that question, even for a moment, in the back of their minds.

Trying to get back to sleep was futile so he walked through the spacious condo that overlooked Pacific Heights. There was a view from every angle of his bedroom and living room. He went to the kitchen and opened the refrigerator, looking for something that might appeal to him. Nothing did, but he poured himself a glass of orange juice just to be in a moment where something felt normal. Lately, his life had been as surreal as when he was in New York. It was like someone suddenly decided to shine a spotlight on his life and he for one was not pleased with what was being revealed.

Sipping the orange juice, he walked to the living room and reclined on the sectional sofa. It was too quiet and he knew there would be nothing on television so he grabbed the remote and switched on his CD player.

After a second or two of soft whirring sounds, his favorite slow tune came through the JM Lab speakers with perfect clarity. Boyz II Men crooned *How do I...*

The song had never affected Ted as it did now. He had always liked this song for different reasons. Clearly the lyrics indicated that it was a goodbye song. Many times after he had made love to a woman and wanted to break up with her, he would play this song.

After such an intimate moment, they thought it a mere romantic gesture. That is, until he told them to get dressed and find their own way home. It wasn't that he was heartless; it was that these individuals had it coming.

The song, still a goodbye song, now struck a harsh chord of finality. Death was much more real and immediate than ever before. He had played a hand with the devil and lost...big time. There was a lot of truth to the saying that if you can't stand the heat then you should get out of the kitchen. Ted had always known if he kept playing with fire, he would get burned. The truth was, the worst he ever bargained on was Herpes.

He reflected on the seven people he had to break the horrible news to. It had not been easy for any of them. They all reacted differently, but in the end there were mostly tears. Ted had not felt the urge to cry about his situation even once.

They would have never given him the time of day if he had not revealed that he headed up his own musical software firm. They were gold diggers, plain and simple.

It did not make breaking the news to them any easier. By law and under the strict enforcement of the Center for Disease Control and the Department of Public Health, he had to tell all the people he had been intimate with that they risked infection.

Ted was bitter. What about the person that infected him? He was not sure that one of the people he had told was not the person who infected him.

Monica was an around-the-way girl who reminded Ted a lot of himself. She was direct and most of the time just plain rude. A secretary at one of the investment firms he and Devin were in talks with a few years back, Ted put forth more effort than he should have in winning her over. Her skin was the color of cinnamon and smoother than silk. Usually a woman's aspirations had to exceed being a secretary for him, but what she lacked in career ambition, she more than made up for in the bedroom. The girl had a voracious appetite for sex and was one of the few who could match his libido pound for pound.

Monica promised to "blow his brains out" if she ever seen him on the street. Fortunately, she lived a two-hour drive away so Ted did not feel that he was in any immediate danger.

Debbie never asked any questions. He could be gone for months, show up at her doorstep unannounced and still be greeted with open legs. She was crazy like that but also desperate to have a little mixed baby boy. She was Philippina but believed in the Chinese fertility calendar. She knew she could give Ted a son whenever he was ready. There was only one problem. He was never going to be ready for a woman to have a permanent leash around his neck. Their escapades always began with a massage. The massages were the best he had ever had and she knew it. When she thought she had Ted at his weakest, she would mount him and try to get him to impregnate her.

He was always prepared during those times with a Trojan. Debbie was the only person he ever occasionally used protection with. He knew Debbie's cycle better than she did and knew when protection was needed and when it wasn't. The Chinese fertility calendar had nothing on him.

Debbie cursed him out and for the first time spoke in her native tongue. He did not understand one word of the Filipino language, but he knew that he did not have to. The venom in her foreign words required no translation.

Eileene was what could be commonly referred to as an undercover freak. She did things with her mouth that would put the pros to shame but she had that lily-white persona working in her favor. Her husband was some big shot Senior Vice President at a Fortune 500 company, who in Ted's opinion had no ability to satisfy his wife. She had been after Ted since she first seen him in the bank. A brother in a suit, transferring large sums of money from one account to another was a turn on for any woman, black, white or green. Ted took delight in breaking down her facade of prejudice. He eventually learned after one of their urgent love making sessions that she was one of the most liberal Caucasians, male or female, that he had ever met.

As she traced languid circles on his bare chest, she confessed secrets to him that she had told no one. Tales of racist parents who were committed to keeping their bloodline pure made Ted sick to his stomach. Eileene's brother began dating a young, Black woman and spoke of marrying her. The news sent the family into a tailspin. When the woman was found dead in her apartment of an apparent suicide, everyone knew what had happened, but no one spoke a word.

It sounded like something out of an old movie. Ted was shocked people could get away with things like that. The notion was ridiculous. Everyone knew Blacks did not commit suicide, at least not intentionally.

Ted's devastating news had crushed Eileene. She now had the terrible burden of breaking the news to her husband.

"I should have listened to my father," was her only comment.

Thandi was very much into her blackness. The dreadlocks she wore were always neat and orderly. The fashionable clothing, though always ethnic, accented by her shapely figure. She decorated her bungalow-style home with African artifacts and motifs in every room. She ate only organic foods and

believed solely in the holistic approach to healing. Her mantra was that her body was a temple. Ted was helpless to argue the point. She had the body and endurance of a track star. The mere scent of her brought Ted's manhood to full attention. What he liked most about Thandi was that he knew she had no interest in his money. She appreciated his forthrightness and the simple pleasures in life. Although she had a boyfriend, Ted appreciated that she just let him be who and what he was. Unfortunately, it had cost her. Thandi was cool, calm and collected when she told him she would pray for his slow and painful death.

Tracey was a beautiful woman with skin the color of Sue B. Honey. She had shoulder-length hair that she rarely wore down, unless she was seeing Ted. Her tall, shapely frame gave her the appearance of a model. If Ted had been the marrying kind, Tracey is the one he would have brought home to meet his mother. She was intelligent and strong while being shy and demure.

She never raised her voice because there had never been a need to. Ted felt completely comfortable in her company. In fact, in many instances, he felt more comfortable at her home than he did his own. Although she never pressured him, he knew she wanted to get married and have children before she reached thirty-eight.

Tracey was an editor for a major Bay Area newspaper and ran her own editorial services company on the side. Ted wished he had it in him to settle down. If he had married Tracey he knew his life would have had a much happier ending. Having to break the news to Tracey was bad enough, but her reaction cut him deep.

"I think I'm pregnant," she stated simply.

Hers was a blessing and a curse. It seemed her prayer of becoming pregnant had been answered, but with grave consequences. Ted shook his head. He was not in any shape to deal with this now or ever. Tracey curled up under her covers, the very covers where they had made love numerous times before and cried like a baby all the while asking him why? Sadly, he did not have an answer. He walked out of her door and out of her life, hoping for both their sakes that he would never see her again. Unfortunately, she had become involved with the wrong man...him.

Mikaela was a high-maintenance, high yellow, woman who wanted desperately to be somebody important. The fact that she was no more than a ghetto queen living on Section 8 housing did not deflate her ego one bit. She had three kids, the youngest of whom she maintained was Ted's but a paternity test and the distinct similarity between the child and her ex-boyfriend blew holes in that theory. That had been a close call and Ted was relieved that he had dodged that bullet. He would gladly trade situations now.

Men were attracted to Mikaela because she appeared to be a conquest. The truth was, she was an easy capture if you flashed a little money. Ted was still confused as to why he kept her on the roster. She was baggage to any man. While the sex was good, he had certainly had better. In the end, he guessed he was in it for the conquest too. Although it did not seem possible, Mikaela's life would take a turn for the worse because of him.

He had to give it to Mikaela, she was a trooper. The first question she asked when he told her that she needed to get tested was, "What symptoms do you have?" He did not bother to go into the details with her. She then hauled off and slapped him.

"I got three kids. What am I supposed to do?" she demanded.

She was the only one he apologized to. After all, one of those kids could have been his.

This next individual he had become involved with during a fleeting moment of drunkenness and weakness. He had always heard people refer to a drunk speaking a sober mind. He guessed it was true because he could not deny that he had thought about it before. His pride told him that he was a ladies man to the end. He loved the touch and feel of a woman's breasts pressed up against him, the softness of her skin, the very scent of her. But the truth called him a liar the morning he woke up next to Khalil.

Khalil was a slightly younger, fit, attractive brother who sported dreadlocks. He was a web developer for a software firm whose future looked promising. They originally met in passing at a bar where Ted was to meet some potential investors. The investors called Ted on his cell phone and cancelled. Ted and Khalil began talking about women. He respected the brother because he knew they were alike. Women were staking their claim on both of them all night. In the end, they collected several phone numbers each, but left together.

Fortunately, Ted was able to call Devin and tell him not to come. Ted was sure that Devin being there would have only prolonged the inevitable. For Ted, Khalil was a diversion from himself. The thought of having sex with a man had always seemed safe when wrapped in the confines of his mind. Part of the attraction was having control and the other part was having variety.

Khalil had not taken the news any better than the women he told.

"What nigga?" was all Ted heard. Khalil kicked and threw things around his apartment and then out of nowhere threw a punch that landed right on Ted's jaw.

To take him and mop the floor up with him was futile. He understood what Khalil and everybody else was feeling. Eerily enough, there were at least twelve others who he had come in contact with over the past year alone. If he included his business trips that number would double. Yet, he had no way of contacting them now even if he wanted to.

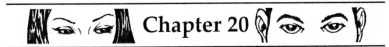

Chapter 20

One year later...

Taylor sat at a small table for two drinking tea at a local Starbuck's. She felt better than she had in a long time. She took another sip of her Chai tea and glanced around the fashionable coffeehouse. On a lazy Saturday morning, the establishment had been scarcely populated but was filing up fast.

Camara sat down in the chair opposite Taylor and handed her a cinnamon scone. "You know this is really nice. We haven't done this in such a long time," Camara said.

"I know. We're always just so busy. I'm learning to better manage my personal time though. I'm so glad you introduced me to this tea, girl. It's all I drink these days."

"And much better for you than coffee. You're really looking like the old Taylor I remember."

"I'll take that as a compliment. It's funny. The truth is that things are far from perfect, but I am different. I've really begun to put things in perspective. Things will probably never be perfect. No one's life is. But for once, I'm completely okay with that. I just need some things to at least be workable instead of broken all the time."

Camara nodded her head in agreement.

"I hear 'ya. All I know is that I'm really glad you're no longer taking those pills. What were you thinking? I was really worried about you for a minute there. I just felt like I had somehow failed you as a friend. We have talked about everything under the sun. Many times it's like we can read each other's thoughts. This time we were obviously both out of sync or something because I had no idea that there was anything wrong."

"You know Cam, it's been a journey. The past two years have been the worst of my life, both personally and professionally. I can't ever remember feeling more alone despite having the company of family and friends. It all started with feeling overwhelmed and snowballed from there."

"Was it that bad?"

"Yeah; worse actually. Imagine having two kids and having to play mommy and daddy to both of them because your husband is never around. And to top it off, he's only helping minimally financially because all his money is tied up in his business. But you know, I probably could've dealt with all that just fine had it not been for the infidelity factor."

"Ouch!" Camara grimaced as she began to grasp a glimpse of what her friend had been enduring.

Taylor nodded her head and blinked back the impending onslaught of tears.

"Look, we've talked about this before. It's a beautiful day. Why don't we take advantage of this opportunity and head to Nordstrom's," Camara offered.

Taylor laughed and dabbed at her eyes.

"You're a better friend than you give yourself credit for Camara. You didn't miss anything with me. I hid it really well...I became a master at that. Of course then, you had a tragedy in your life as well. I should have been a better friend to you during that time."

Now it was Camara's turn to dab at her eyes. "What are

you talking about, you were at the funeral."

"I know, but you needed me more and my head was somewhere in the clouds. I think we both needed this talk for different reasons."

"Yeah, me too," Camara responded, her voice somewhere in the distance. "Bottom line Taye, I see an improvement in Devin. He's definitely with the boys more, giving you a little more down time."

"Yeah."

"Do you think he's still seeing someone?"

"I don't know. What I'm most concerned about is whether I'll ever trust him again...they way I used to."

"Take it from me. You'll never trust any man again the way you might have before. It's just a woman's defense mechanism that kicks in once we've been hurt before."

"I'm sure you're right. The only problem is that it's my husband and I still love him."

"And he loves you too, Taylor. Otherwise you would never see any improvement in his behavior. You two have been together for so long and it would devastate Jr. and Chaz."

Taylor shot her friend an impatient look.

"I know, I know. Children are not the only reason why a couple should stay together, but they're a good reason, especially when there's so much time already invested."

"I know. Don't get me wrong I haven't run out and filed divorce papers or anything. I just want to be treated like a wife is supposed to be."

"Do you know for sure that Devin had an affair?"

"Like I know the sun will rise in the morning. Camara, now you're insulting my intelligence," Taylor's voice shrieked.

"If you're asking me have I seen him in the act, the answer is no. Have I found any incriminating evidence? The answer is yes because you know I had him investigated. I needed to know beyond the shadow of a doubt that he was being unfaithful. He's told me about these "business meetings" that go into the wee hours of the night where there is very little business conducted and far more socializing."

"And?"

"And what?"

"Just because he told you about the meetings doesn't mean he's had an affair."

"No, the proof from the private investigator means he's had an affair. I just stopped the investigation because I couldn't take knowing any more. Look, I know you are the consummate cupid who hopelessly believes in love to the end, but you forget, I work in Corporate America. I know what goes on at these retreats and off-site meetings. You couldn't tell one of their meetings from the inside of a brothel."

"You are too much," Camara said laughing.

"You know I'm telling the truth that's why you're laughing." Taylor said joining in.

"I'm sorry. This really is not a laughing matter. I just know how bad it hurt when I seen my ex get off the plane with his little whore. The thing is, if he is not parading whomever around, allowing them to play wifey when you're not around and you haven't had the displeasure of having to put a face to your accusations, then consider yourself lucky and try to get past it."

"Yeah. I'm trying to do that, but every now and again the mistrust will just come out of nowhere and blind side me. Believe me though, I've done the crying thing, the what did I do wrong thing and I've come to the conclusion that you can't stop a person from doing what they want to do. It wouldn't matter if I were the best and most beautiful wife in the world. The grass always looks greener."

Camara reached out and squeezed her friend's hand.

"Taye, I'm not trying to tell you what to do, but there are so many people out here who don't have anyone or the person they have is so bad, they wish they didn't have anyone. I'm just sayin' don't make more out of it than necessary. Look, I'm not saying he's innocent, I'm just saying make sure that whatever you decide, you give it a lot of thought. Whatever your decision, you must live with it and I support you either way."

"I know what you're sayin' believe me. I do. But 'ya know let's talk about you though. I always get on my soapbox and monopolize the conversation. I have faith that Devin and I will work through this. Now what's been happening with you?"

Camara smiled like she possessed the greatest secret in the world.

"Ooh! Come on, spill it," Taylor urged.

"Spill what?" Camara smiled coyly.

"Don't even go there!"

"Okay. I'll tell you if you come to Nordy's with me."

"Color me there, 'cause I can tell this is going to be good."

The two women cleared their table and walked out into the warm mid-morning sun where they headed for Camara's two-seater BMW.

Once inside the cozy sports car Camara popped in her Jill Scott CD and headed for Highway 101. Jill Scott's soulful voice crooned *The Way* in the background.

"Okay, enough with the stalling, let's have it," Taylor demanded.

"All right, all right. I guess I've made you wait long enough. Well, I met this guy."

"Ooooooh. Okay what's his name?"

"Would you let me finish? My goodness! His name is Randolph Cellars."

"Wait a minute. Randolph Cellars?"

"Yes." Camara replied looking straight ahead at the road.

"Hmmm. Okay."

"And he's the most romantic, sensitive man I've ever met."

"Well when did you meet him?"

"A few months ago. It's been really great. It's not like I live this sheltered life or anything, but he has taken me to all these little secret restaurants and art galleries that I never knew existed."

"Okay now I have to ask this question. Is he Black?"

"No."

"I knew it. When you mentioned the art galleries I had this feeling we were not dealing with your average brotha'."

"So you're not shocked?"

"Why would I be? I mean it's one of those things that are becoming more and more prevalent. We see Black men with White women all day long. The important thing is being with someone who treats you right and makes you happy. I can't wait to meet this Mr. Cellars. He sounds like some wealthy aristocrat with a name like that."

"I don't think he's rich, but he seems to be financially sound. He owns a couple of commercial properties in the Financial District."

"I'm impressed," Taylor said arching one of her brows. "What does he do for a living?"

"He's a contractor."

"Okay, now I see the connection."

"His nose is not as up in the air as his name might lead you to believe. Everybody calls him Randy and he's very much a Polo shirt and khakis type of guy."

"You go girl!"

"I'm trying. I know it's only been a short while, but I really like him. It's amazing that you can go through your entire life thinking that you've experienced what's good and then some body or something comes along and really shows you what it's like to live and be loved."

"Wow! Already talking the big "L" word," Taylor teased.

"It's still early, but you know how you get butterflies in your stomach when you talk to someone you care about on the phone? When we go out to dinner, I hardly have an appetite because I'm full on the words he speaks to me."

Taylor pondered what her friend was saying. She definitely remembered what that feeling was like and she missed it. She looked at her friend as she spoke of this alleged Prince Charming. Taylor was genuinely happy for her. It had been a long time since she had dated anyone after her divorce.

"Camara that's really great. I'm happy for you. I hope it works out and blossoms into something beautiful for you."

"Well, like I said, it's still early, but who knows. Right now it's just nice to share the company of a man again. Particularly a man that seems to be as interested in me as I am in him."

"So what does Randy look like?"

"He reminds me of Matt Damon, sort of."

"Okay now!"

"He's about 6'1 and physically fit. He runs five miles a day and plays tennis in his spare time."

"You mean he doesn't play golf?" Taylor joked.

"See, you ain't right. Tiger Woods proves that golf is not just for our lighter skinned counterparts."

"I know that, girl. Let's not forget Venus and Serena Williams too. They've got the tennis thing down," Taylor joked. "But seriously, I'm really glad for you. Now you know I have to ask. What's it like?"

"What is what like?" Camara asked pretending not to know what her friend was asking as she took the 19th Avenue Exit off the freeway.

Anna Dennis

"Don't play dumb with me. You know exactly what I'm talking about. What's he like in bed?"

"Look at you! All in the Kool-Aid."

"That's right, now start pouring 'cause I already know the flavor."

Camara started laughing so hard she missed the light signaling her turn and the car behind her responded with a furious blaring of its horn. When the arrow light turned green again Camara turned into the parking garage of Nordstrom.

Because it was still early in the day, she found a parking spot without any effort. She pulled into the stall and cut off the engine.

"Okay," Camara said still giggling from Taylor's comment. "I'll just say this. What they say about white men is totally untrue."

They two women gave each other a high-five and headed into the shopping center.

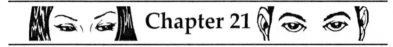 **Chapter 21**

Devin sat at the conference table along with Ted and eight of their investors. Fortunately, Mymelody.com's forecast was looking solid for the current quarter and beyond. They were two hours into their three-hour meeting. They had covered all the agenda topics but had come back around to the subjects of budget and ensuring the features on the site were competitive with similar sites that had recently been launched.

"Currently we're in the black which is good given the economy since September 11 last year. We all know that start-ups in the area have been hit incredibly hard. We should all be proud in keeping ourselves afloat," Mr. McFadden said as he scanned the documents in front of him."

"Absolutely," Mr. Barron agreed.

"But what is our projected five-year profit margin? As websites and its users become savvier so too will the ability to download music. How can Mymelody.com remain competitive and keep its customers?" Mr. Fordham asked directing his question to Ted.

During their pre-meeting briefing, Devin noticed Ted had been a little out of sorts. They attempted to cover all bases and anticipate all potential questions that might be asked of them.

All the investors knew Devin was the numbers man and Ted was the pitchman, but it was not uncharacteristic of Fordham to test their knowledge of the others expertise. Devin hoped his partner would be able to pull it together during the meeting. So far, he had been pensive and reflective. Devin waited to see his reply to Mr. Fordham's question.

"Well, things are looking good going forward. We project that we will easily be in the black for the next five years at our current rate," Ted replied.

Devin squeezed the bridge of his nose and sighed quietly. They had just gone over the numbers not more than two hours ago and now here Ted was giving this generic response.

"Additionally, we will continue to enhance and upgrade each model we release," Ted continued.

"It's good to know the company will still be around in five years Ted, but can you give me specifics?"

"Maybe I didn't provide Ted with the same sheet I have," Devin interjected. " I actually did the flow chart for the five-year projectory. In two years Mymelody.com should see a net profit of about 5 million dollars, the number will actually be reduced to 3.7 million after deducting operating expenses. However, we should slightly more than double that in five years," Devin concluded, distributing copies of his graph to the investors.

"Impressive," Mr. Matthews chimed in.

"Thank you. We plan to kick-off a promotional campaign and work with various radio stations and internet providers to direct traffic to our site. We will launch our promotional campaign in phases and as Ted mentioned, we will upgrade products and services with each release. Conducting the process this way will give us the opportunity to learn from the feedback we receive and target any areas of concern."

"How many phases do you anticipate?" Mr. Hervey

asked.

"Three within a twelve month time period beginning in January."

"Mymelody.com has been in existence for almost two years. Do you think this whole...uh, re-launch will make customers wary?" Mr. McFadden asked.

Devin took note that the same five investors had been asking all the questions. Three had not asked one question since the start of the meeting. They merely sat and agreed or disagreed with the majority. An occasional nod of the head showed Devin they would swing with whatever the majority decided.

Devin glanced at Ted who seemed to be having trouble focusing. Sweat glistened above his brow and Devin noticed his shallow, rapid breathing. He wondered if anyone else had noticed.

"Okay. Well, I think that does it for me," Mr. McFadden said, leading the charge once again.

"Thank you gentlemen," Devin said standing from his chair.

"Yeah, thanks gentlemen," Ted said shaking a few hands and making a quick exit.

After the investors left, Devin made his way to Ted's office. He found him in his office sitting on the edge of his sofa. He looked like he was about to pass out. Devin rushed to Ted's side.

"Whoah man! What's going on? Are you alright?"

"Dev man, I need you to get me to a hospital," Ted said weakly.

"Should I call 9-1-1?"

"No. I just need you to get me outta here man."

"Okay, okay. Can you make it through the lobby?"

"I think so."

Devin managed to help Ted to his feet. He had no idea

what was going on, but he understood that Ted was trying to be strong about it. As a man he knew there would be no honor in being carried out on a stretcher from his own establishment.

Fortunately, it was the lunch hour and the office staff was scarce. Everyone on their seven-person staff seemed to be out except for one lead business developer and the receptionist.

Devin straightened Ted's tie and wiped his face with his handkerchief. Ted seemed to be getting worse, but composed himself as much as he could when they walked through the reception area.

"Is everything okay Mr. Harris," the receptionist asked.

"Everything is fine Marjorie. Mr. Levingston and I should return in a couple of hours," Devin lied. His priority was to honor his friend's request and get him out of the office with his dignity in tact and then to find out exactly what was going on.

Devin sat in the emergency room of the hospital waiting to find out what was wrong with his friend.

Ted had been admitted almost two hours ago and no one had been able to give any updates as to his condition. Devin despised the processes hospitals had in place. All the paper work required before you could even be seen made his stomach turn. He wondered if a study had ever been done on how many people actually died in the emergency room while waiting to be seen.

"Mr. Harris?" Devin heard, being pulled from his cynical thoughts.

"Yes," he said standing and walking toward the thin, Hispanic doctor.

"Hello, I'm Dr. Pader are you Mr. Levinston's next of

kin?"

Another process I hate, Devin thought. "Yes, he's my cousin," Devin responded.

"Okay, why don't we step over here for a minute," Dr. Pader suggested. They walked over to a less populated area near the nurses' station. Dr. Pader opened Ted's chart and began flipping through the documents as if seeing them for the first time.

"Well, this is what we have here. Ted has a host of things going on right now. What's causing his extreme fatigue, fever and weakness is the Pneumococcal Pneumonia. I'm not his regular physician, but according to the information in his chart he has sustained a substantial weight loss over the past few months as well. He also has early signs of developing oral hairy leukoplakia. All of this we can treat with antibiotics and Prednisone or Zidovudine to get him better for now. What we're most concerned with now is his low CD4 count, which is just slightly above 350."

"Wait a minute! Just stop! What are you telling me? I...I mean I'm no doctor, but I recognize some of these terms and you must be talking about somebody else. Maybe you've got his chart mixed up or something."

Dr. Pader stood looking perplexed for a moment, the realization slowly sinking in. "I'm sorry. I guess you weren't made aware of the nature of Mr. Levingston's illness."

"Humph! You're right, I wasn't made aware and I don't want to hear anymore about this. Where is Ted? Can I see him?"

"Sure, just check with one of the nurses so that you can get a surgical mask before going in."

Devin felt like the wind had just been knocked out of him. This was too much to deal with at once. He needed to see Ted and get this thing cleared up. There had to be some sort of misunderstanding. He checked in at the nurses' station and received his surgical mask.

"Right down the hall and to your right. Room number 14," the nurse announced.

Devin's feet felt like lead. Part of him wanted to turn and run in the opposite direction and the other part of him wanted to turn back time so that the details of the past ten minutes could really sink in. He reached room number 14 and stopped dead in his tracks. Although he had seen his friend a little over two hours ago, he was afraid of what he would see on the other side of the door. It was clear that secrets had been kept, understandably, but he could not get his mind around how to respond to this horrible turn of events.

He took a deep breath, thankful for the mask that at least covered half of his face. He wished it could cover his entire face right now and shield him from the terrible truth he knew was on the other side of the door. He walked into the semi-private room. Fortunately, Ted was the only person in the room.

He appeared to be sleeping. Devin noticed the oxygen tubes going into his nose and the IV into his arm. He also noticed the purple blotches on his arms and neck that had been covered by his shirt and coat earlier. Devin squeezed his eyes shut and took another deep breath before proceeding. Just as he reached Ted's bedside, Ted turned and looked directly at him. Devin froze.

"I bet you never thought you'd see your boy like this, huh?" Ted managed, his voice sounding slightly distorted.

"Man...what's going on Ted? How could you let this happen?"

"You know me...I believe in living life to the fullest," Ted replied making a feeble attempt at humor. It was lost on Devin.

"Don't joke about this. I thought you stayed strapped."

"You know how that is man. Sometime you do, sometimes you don't. More often than not, I didn't."

"Why didn't you tell me about this...that you had HIV.

You had to have known for a while man. Why didn't you let me help you?"

"Help me? When did you add Ph.D. to your name?" Ted asked, his voice taking on a more morbid tone. "I didn't know about this until recently. Sure I suspected, but part of me didn't want to know. Haven't you heard? AIDS kills; there is no cure. Man, I can't lie. This is hell, uncut no chaser and it's only going to get worse. I know this. I also know that when you make your bed you gotta' lay in it. You know me Dev. I wouldn't change one thing about my life or its ending. Men envied me and I couldn't blame 'em. So what's the point now in feeling all sorry for myself...putting this burden on you to feel sorry for me. I'm not going out like that."

"Well what are the doctor's telling you?

"What is there to tell me? The prognosis is bleak. Right now, it's HIV, but it will get worse. I will get AIDS...the question is not if. The question is when?"

"How long have you known, Ted?" Devin asked as he turned his back to Ted and stared out the window at the darkening skyline.

"A little over a year," Ted replied.

"So," Devin said, turning to face his friend again. "What was the plan...just die and not let anyone in on it? Not tell 'ya boy?" Devin asked as his indignation rose.

"If I was lucky," Ted replied solemnly. "Dev, man, you have no idea what it's like to deal with this," Ted managed between ragged breaths. "I thought about telling you, but my pride wouldn't let me. I hate to say it, but I wouldn't have told anyone if I had my choice. I just wanted to live as best I could for as long as I could."

"I can't believe this," Devin said rubbing his head. "You're right, I don't have any idea. I didn't mean to come down on you like that. What do you want me to tell the office...the investors?"

"Tell them I have pneumonia. It's the truth ain't it?"

"Yeah, it's the truth." Devin said turning away again.

He was not about to make Ted say it. To admit his biggest fear...that he would most likely never come back to the office again.

"Well just tell me what you need me to take care of and I'll do it." Devin desperately wanted to change the tone of the conversation to something less morbid.

"I'm not worried about the office. You know the business as well as I do. Do what you need to do. You're the only family I got so I want you to set up a living trust for me immediately and then act as my trustee."

"Ted you gotta be kidding me. I'm not an attorney."

"You don't have to be. Look consult whomever you want or need to, but I want you running things."

"Ted, this is not a death sentence. Yes, you're sick now, but I know they're giving you antibiotics and you'll be better in a week or so."

"Yeah but for how long? And I definitely won't be well enough to work full-time. I can't predict when I'll get sick again or where and I won't go back to the company like this. I have a reputation to uphold. After a couple of weeks, just tell everyone I've taken a sabbatical."

"Look, I'll consult as long as I can, but look at me. I just need to get my affairs in order and I need your help."

"You got it."

"Thanks man."

Devin did not know how to respond to his newly appointed position. It was unsettling and foreign. It went beyond Ted being sick. It seemed death clung in the air around Ted. What disturbed him more was Ted seemed ready to welcome it. Devin felt a twist deep in his gut. He and Ted had been like brothers since college. He could not remember any significant event in his life where Ted did not play an integral part.

Clearly that was going to change. He was more afraid than he could ever remember being.

"Look you take care of yourself and I'll check back with you in a couple of days," Devin said, patting Ted on the shoulder. He turned to leave.

"All right. Hey Dev, one last thing?"

"What's that?"

"Don't let anyone at the office know. Promise me that."

Devin paused for a moment and looked at his friend. Ted had lost more weight but even with the oxygen tubes in his nose, he still looked healthy...like the Ted Devin had always known. Devin surmised that maybe it was what he wanted to see. He wanted to remember his friend that way; the smooth talking salesman and ladies man. "You know your secret is safe with me." Devin turned and walked out of the hospital room before the stinging sensation in his eyes became too telling.

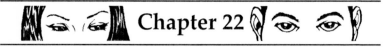 **Chapter 22**

Taylor sat on the edge of her bed rummaging through her nightstand. While talking on the phone to her mother earlier, the back to one of her pearl earrings had fallen into the drawer. She and her mother had not really had a long conversation in months. Today had been like old times. Taylor had not realized how much she missed the conversations with her mother. They talked about everything under the sun right up to Christmas dinner plans at the Harris household. She had fifteen minutes to get ready before Devin began badgering her about being late.

She had finally gotten Devin to agree to going out. It had required some real effort on her part, but persistence had paid off. The boys were staying overnight again with neighbors, who had two sons between the ages of Devin Jr. and Chaz. When Devin and Taylor first moved to the neighborhood she and Vicky hit it off right away. Vicky was six years older than Taylor and loved kids. At one point, each of them took turns babysitting each other's boys, but Taylor knew the Simons were having their share of family struggles here and there too because her husband was a workaholic. She and Vicky Simons had renewed their agreement to help the other out to spend quality time with their husbands. She knew she owed Vicky a few evenings alone with her husband.

Things seemed to have picked up at work for Devin. He had been working twelve to fourteen hour days for the past few weeks and he needed a break whether he believed it or not. She was glad he had not needed to travel lately. His traveling always brought back her feelings of insecurity, particularly when traveling with Ted.

Devin appeared preoccupied lately. She new there had to be something going on at the office that had him stressed out. During times like this, he often retreated to the point of becoming reclusive.

Their marriage had it shares of tumultuous times, but as the holidays approached, she was making a commitment to get her relationship back on track and in a healthy state before the New Year. She thought back to her conversation with Camara. The fact that she had proof of Devin's affair and still allowed him in her bed would make her look like the fool in the eyes of many, except her mom. Being from the old school, her mom believed marriage was forever, but she also recognized that it was not easy being alone.

"As long as he comes back to the home he takes care of is all that matters," she had told Taylor.

On one of he and Ted's business trips, she hired a private investigator to follow Devin. She made sure to provide the investigator with all the details she could to make his job easier. She provided all the logistics she could gather. At first she had second thoughts. Part of her had to know and the other part wanted desperately to run from the truth...run and hide. In the end, knowing had not changed a thing. In fact, it made things that much more complicated.

She rationalized that at least Devin was not in a long-term relationship. Therefore, it could really not be considered an affair. Plus, she only had proof of one incident.

Taylor froze when she came across an old prescription bottle containing three Xanax. She picked up the bottle and stared at its content as if she were afraid of it. She went to the bathroom opened the bottle and flushed the pills down the toilet.

She went back to the edge of the bed a little shaken. It had been months since she had taken a sleeping pill or even an aspirin for that matter. To see a reminder of a very dark period in her life that was still so fresh, really scared her. She located the back to her earring and quickly fastened it. She then slipped into her strapless, black dress lying on the bed. All she had left to do was put on the finishing touches of her make-up. She switched on the portable CD player. Mary J. Blige's *Love Without A Limit* came through, providing the mood music she needed right now.

Applying her mascara, eyeliner and shadow, within minutes, Taylor's face looked flawless. She smoothed her hair on the sides and pulled it up into a bun high atop her head, securing it with a diamond, butterfly clip. She then accented the style by leaving curly tendrils here and there.

She thought she heard Devin making his way up the stairs, but before she could confirm her suspicions, Devin was standing right behind her, close. He wrapped his arms around her waist and pressed even closer. She could feel his arousal. He unzipped the dress, which slid unheeded to the floor, then cupped her firm breasts in each of his hands. She sighed with pleasure.

"Devin I was ready to leave."

"Shhhh," he interrupted. "Don't worry," he continued, gently kissing the nape of her neck.

"Ooooh Devin. We're going to be late for our dinner reservations," Taylor sighed.

"Dinner can wait. I'm hungry for something else," Devin replied unfastening Taylor's bra and turning her to face him. He then removed the diamond clip from her hair allowing her dark brown tresses to fall freely to her shoulders.

Devin kissed her passionately and eased her back on the bed. Taylor slid off his dinner jacket and unbuttoned his shirt.

Her hands conducted their own exploration of his body as she caressed his arms, chest and throbbing member. He slid Taylor's panties down with his index finger and tossed them aside while she unfastened his slacks. Their kisses became urgent and hungry. It had been a long time since Devin had truly made love to her. He explored every part of her body as if re-familiarizing himself with its shape and contours. He continued his exploration from Taylor's breasts to below her waist for a long while until Taylor begged and pleaded for him to have her. When he began, his strokes were deep, slow and deliberate.

He wanted to please her physically and mentally and banish the veil of insecurity that he knew had been created over the years.

Taylor's mind vacillated somewhere between fantasy, reality and ecstasy. Her hands gathered bunches of the silk duvet and clutched it fiercely. Her mind felt free of doubt and her body weightless...almost numb, with the exception of the pulsating pleasure she felt radiating from in between her legs to her lower stomach. Just when she thought she might scream, Devin captured her lips with his mouth, ravaging her tongue with his own. For now, all fear and insecurities were buried somewhere in the recesses of her mind. She was made safe in the embrace of her husband's arms.

His strokes became faster but no less deliberate and intense.

They moaned together signaling the impending climax that they both eagerly awaited, yet wished would never come to pass.

Devin and Taylor were over an hour late for their reservation. With a little persuasion and a large tip, the maitrd' was able to accommodate them with a table for two that overlooked the beautiful San Francisco Bay. The expansive Bay Bridge stretched out before them making it appear as if they could open the window and walk out on the upper deck of the bridge. Alcatraz and Treasure Islands provided a beatific backdrop to the scenery. They were both famished. Taylor ordered the chicken pasta primavera with the house salad and Devin ordered the half-pound prime rib with au jus, mashed potatoes and vegetables. When their orders came, they were finished eating in less than half an hour and ready for dessert. Taylor smiled seductively across the table at her husband, thinking back to their lovemaking sessions not more than an hour ago.

"Beautiful isn't it?" Taylor said, taking in the décor of the restaurant. The colors were warm, bronze and burgundy earth tones with suede tapestry that adorned the walls. A red rose accented each table and the candlelight added to the intimacy and ambiance of the restaurant.

"Yeah, the view isn't bad either," Devin responded smiling back at his wife. "I think we need this Devin. We need more us time."

"I agree baby. It just seems that over the years, it's gotten so hard to find time. There always seems to be something going on. But, I do hear what you're saying and we need to make a commitment that will keep us on track."

"You don't know how glad it makes me to hear you say that. I don't know what's going on, but I like it."

"Well, there's been a lot going on. I hope I don't dampen the mood when I tell you this, but better now than when it's too late."

"Tell me what? I mean I knew something was going on because it seems like you've been in the Twilight Zone for the past few weeks."

"The Twilight Zone would be a sweet reprieve from what I've been going through. No joke! It's been crazy and then some."

"What is it?" Taylor asked with growing concern.

"Look Taye, I know how you feel about Ted but..."

"Okay, I really don't want to talk about Ted. I know he's you're boy and all, but this has been a really good night and I don't want to ruin it," Taylor said, grimacing.

"Please let me finish. Look, I started not to say anything, but this is serious and it's not going to get any better. It's not solely about Ted, it's about the company and I need your support."

"I'm sorry. " Taylor's brow furrowed with concern. "Go ahead."

"I've been really bogged down at the office for the past several weeks because I've been the only one there."

"What do you mean you've been the only one there? Where is everyone?"

"Well, I mean the staff has been there, but Ted has been out for the past few weeks. I've been carrying both our workloads."

"Why? What's going on?"

"Ted has HIV." Devin said solemnly.

"What?" Taylor gasped.

"Yeah and I don't know how things are gonna play out for him."

"What do you mean? It's horrible, but people don't necessarily die from HIV."

"That's true, but I don't know how long he's had it. He told me he's only known for about a year."

"And what? You don't believe him?"

"I don't know what to believe. It's all so bizarre. You just never think things like this will hit so close to home."

"I hate to sound so callous but with Ted's behavior, are you really surprised?"

"Of course I am. This is not like catching a cold or something, Taylor," Devin responded incredulously.

"You're right. It's really unfortunate for him and the women he's come in contact with. Do you know how many women that might be?"

"No, but then we haven't had that conversation either. I don't feel like I'm getting the full story from him anyway, 'ya know?"

"I bet. It's a disease that comes with a lot of shame no matter how one contracts the virus. Did he tell you?"

"No and I didn't ask. I know he doesn't do drugs...I just don't know, but it's not hard to figure out."

"Devin I'm really sorry about Ted. I wouldn't wish that on anyone, but when you lead a certain lifestyle, there are consequences that come as a result of your actions."

"Taylor please try and stay with me. We both know that you don't like Ted."

"That would be putting it mildly," Taylor interrupted.

"What is it with you?"

"Do you really need to ask?" Taylor asked, her voice raising an octave.

"Look are you going to get off your soap box long enough to hear me out or not?"

"Devin I will support you no matter what, you know that. But you need to hear me out too. Like I said, what's happening to Ted is bad, but don't expect for me to get all emotional about it. In my honest opinion, he's been a threat to my marriage ever since I've known him."

Devin blew out an exasperated breath. "Taylor, what are

you talking about?"

"He has never respected our marriage. He did things and included you as if you were some single bachelor with no family."

"Taylor I'm a grown man. No one can make me do anything I don't want to do."

"You know what Devin, you're right. I shouldn't blame Ted for what you've done. Maybe I should thank him for allowing me to see what I was really dealing with. What gives Devin? Do you have to contract HIV and give it to me before you can acknowledge that you've been wrong?"

The waitress came and took their plates, interrupting Devin's response.

"And will you two be having dessert this evening," the waitress asked.

"No, but we will take the check," Devin responded sharply. The waitress quickly cleared the table leaving Devin and Taylor in silence.

"You know I really hoped this dinner could be a step in the right direction for us. I needed your support, but before I could even finish telling you what was going on you got started with your own agenda."

Taylor sat in silence fuming. She so wanted this evening to be perfect and now it was turning out completely the opposite. This night was supposed to be a turning point. It had been rough for the past couple of years and this was going to be the evening all that changed. She had once again fell prey to speaking before thinking, but she couldn't help how she felt.

"Devin I..." Taylor began.

"Baby it's okay. I understand that you're bitter. I'm so sorry for that because it's my fault. I've caused this dissention between us, not Ted, and so I need to work on healing us before I ask you about supporting me on anything."

"That's not true," Taylor murmured quietly.

She could tell she had let Devin down. But what about all the times he had let her down? This was not the right time or place to attack him, but before she knew it, the words had already been said. This time, she gauged her words carefully before speaking.

"Devin, I really wanted this evening to work for us too. Every time I think I get past the issues of insecurity and mistrust, I'm proved wrong time and time again."

Devin sat facing the window, but glanced at Taylor intermittently from underneath hooded lids. Taylor hoped he would say something that would let her off the hook, but he didn't. In fact, he never said a word. When the waitress returned with the check, Devin retrieved a one hundred-dollar bill from his wallet and placed it in the tray. He stood. Still a gentleman, he helped Taylor into her wrap and gently guided her in the direction of the door, his hand barely touching the small of her back.

Once outside in the cool night air, Taylor and Devin stood in silence waiting for the valet to bring the car around. A stark contract from the way they had entered the restaurant, hand-in-hand and almost giddy at the simple act of being in each other's company. When the car arrived, Devin opened the door for Taylor and made sure she was situated.

"Devin, I'm sorry."

"Me too," Devin replied and closed the door.

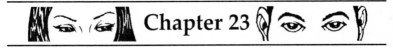 Chapter 23

If the meeting had gone on for another minute, Taylor was going to scream. A one- hour meeting that could have been accomplished in twenty minutes had turned into a two hour and ten minute gripefest. Much like her life, somewhere along the way she had lost control. Although this was a meeting of her peers, her boss had asked her to facilitate the meeting. She honestly could not remember what had been said prior to ten minutes ago. Taylor took a drink of water and glanced at the agenda. The blood rushed to her head when she noticed that they were only halfway through.

"Okay," Taylor spoke, stopping Nancy Hoffman in midsentence. "I really need to wrap this up in the next five minutes. It's almost 12:30 p.m."

"But not more than ten minutes ago, you just told us you didn't mind if we went until 1:00 p.m."

Taylor paused and looked around the room at her coworkers. Four men, one other woman and herself, six in all and of course, the woman had to be the one to remind her that she had erred.

"My apologies Nancy, you must have misunderstood me. When I said I didn't mind if you went until 1:00 p.m., that did not include me. This meeting has continued a lot longer than I expected. I actually have another meeting at 1:00 p.m."

Everyone began gathering his belongings and preparing to leave, except for Nancy. She continued sitting at the large, oval conference table going over the agenda.

"You know there is at least one more topic we need to address before adjourning, Taylor," Nancy said in an almost sing song voice that reminded Taylor of nails scratching against a chalkboard. Everyone seemed to stop what he was doing, except for Martin Falcone. Everyone jokingly called him Marty Falcon the Mafia Boss. He continued gathering up his notepad that only had one sentence written from his morning notes and left.

"Really," Taylor replied smoothly. "And what might that be?"

"The last agenda item refers to our roll out of the new employee benefits package and I believe another draft of that is due tomorrow. As the project lead for that component of the package, it might be best for you to have that discussion sooner rather than later."

"Well unless there has been some significant changes to draft six that I'm not aware of, I believe I'm meeting my timeline for rollout accordingly." Taylor replied coolly.

"As a matter of fact there have been some changes," Nancy said removing her copy of the benefit package from a folder in her planner. Taylor noticed that the document was almost bleeding with red ink. She wondered when the white versus black, power trip thing would end between women in Corporate America. The fact of the matter was that women, either white or black, had to work harder than men to be given the respect a white male received as his due. Unfortunately, that went well beyond the corporate walls and spilled over into everyday life. She was not one to pull the race card and always cry foul, but Nancy was only negative with her and all the time.

There was no way everything she did could be wrong, otherwise she would not be where she was in the company.

"When were these changes made? Taylor asked.

Her right temple began throbbing, but she refused to lose her cool with Nancy.

"Yesterday. I thought we'd have the chance to go over them today, but it doesn't look like that's going to happen," Nancy replied almost too happily for Taylor.

"Why don't you give me the document and I'll have my secretary make the changes."

"Well don't you think we need to go over them?"

By now, there was only one other person from the meeting still there, Fred Warner.

"The document was fine by me Taylor. All my suggestions were turned in last week. I'll see you two later," Fred said heading towards the door of the conference room.

"Thank you Fred. There's really no need to go over them," Taylor said turning to Nancy. "Everyone gave me their recommendations last week and they were implemented into the document. After I make your recommended changes, there will be no more opportunities to make changes unless Jim wants them made. If we are to hit our projected target date we have to draw a line in the sand as to how many times we can go through the revision process."

"I agree," Nancy said much to Taylor's surprise. "We also need to makes sure we're committed going forward on all our rollouts, even if it means rescheduling other meetings or revamping our schedules," Nancy said with a smirk.

Taylor was seeing red and it wasn't just on the paper. If they were both somewhere out on the street and did not work with each other Miss Nancy would be picking herself up off the floor right now. The games people played never ceased to amaze Taylor. Did this woman think Taylor was too stupid to know when she was being insulted or did she just not care? Taylor suspected the latter.

"Your suggestion is duly noted Nancy. In the future, I'll make a concerted effort to accommodate any and all two-hour meetings you decide the team should have," Taylor responded sarcastically.

"Oh no, I wasn't talking about you Taylor. I just meant..."

Taylor walked out of the conference room and strolled down the hall, leaving Nancy exactly where she needed to be, alone.

With only two days left before Thanksgiving Taylor was going to have to burn the midnight oil to get the final draft complete for the following Monday. Normally, she would give this project to her secretary, Karen, but with her boss breathing down her neck, she wanted to make sure she was hands-on with this one. She would need Devin to pick up the boys from school.

That was an uncomfortable thought. She and Devin had not spoken much since their dinner a couple of weeks ago. In retrospect, she wished she had just kept her mouth shut; it would have served for a much better evening and a less stressful existence now. Both of them knew what the problem was and yet, Devin tried to extend the olive branch but she just had to fly off the handle and get her point across. He had been restricting his responses to one-word sentences. Now she was at a loss as to how to make things better again.

She walked back to her office before heading out for her meeting. The first thing she noticed was that her message light was on. She considered checking the messages, but thought better of it. If she got started responding to voice mail, she would surely be late for her next meeting, but before she could put her things down on the desk, her secretary walked in with four message slips.

"Jim left three messages that he needs to see you as soon

as you return," Karen said.

What now? Taylor thought.

"Well, didn't he know I was in the staff planning meeting that he couldn't attend?"

"I told him, but he still called two more times."

"Did he say what it was regarding?"

"No and of course, I didn't ask, he doesn't seem to appreciate that."

"I know," Taylor said taking the messages from Karen.

"Okay, can you call Veronica Peete and tell her I'm running late?"

"Sure thing."

"Oh and can you get started on making these edits to the employee benefits package?"

"No problem."

"Thank you."

Taylor had no choice because of her schedule but to let Karen start the edits. Although she wanted to handhold this project, she had to turn over the reigns for now. She did not know what her boss wanted, but she was sure it meant more work for her. She had to call Devin first and make sure he could pick up the boys.

She hesitantly dialed Devin's office number. To her surprise, he picked up the telephone on the first ring. That usually indicated that he was busy.

"Devin Harris," he answered.

"Hi, it's me."

The phone was silent for a moment.

"Hey, what's going on?"

"Everything and all at once it seems. I need you to pick up the boys this evening. I have a project that I just received a boatload of changes to and they have to be finished and sent up to Jim before the holiday."

"Taylor I've got a million things going on right now. I honestly didn't know when I was going to get home from work this evening."

Taylor was silent.

"Look," Devin continued, "I'll make sure I get the boys, but I may need to come back to the office when you get home."

"Thank you. I'll try to wrap up as soon as I can and then bring what I can home. Oh and Devin?"

"Yeah?"

"I apologize about everything and I love you."

"I love you too," Devin responded, "And I miss us," he added softly.

Taylor's heart soared. She felt like she could conquer whatever lay ahead for her. She knew a mere apology was not going to make things right between them, but it would have to be a start, the start that renewed their spirit and commitment to one another. The old things and past sins would have to be forgiven if they were to ever move forward. The pain ran deep because it was more than just finding out that her husband had been unfaithful; it was learning that her friend, lover and husband of all these years had betrayed her. She loved her husband more than anything in the world, there was no way she could deny that. The pain he had caused her was indescribable but the betrayal was even worse. She wondered if he really had any idea of the affect that he had on her, both positive and negative. When things were good, they were really good and all the former things seemed to never have happened. When things were bad, they were more horrible for her than for him. He was under her skin, in her head and had a stranglehold on her soul. When forced to weigh the plusses and minuses, she would rather have bad times with him than good times alone. Fortunately, their good times together far outweighed the bad. They just needed to get back to that formula and begin to live again.

Taylor gathered her things and headed out the door to meet with her boss.

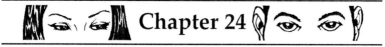 **Chapter 24**

Devin sat quietly in a corner chair at Ted's condominium, glancing back and forth between Ted and the beautiful view of the Golden Gate Bridge. Through the large picture window, it seemed like you could reach out and touch it. He watched as his friend browsed through the legal documents for the planning of his assets and signed in the designated areas. He did not know how he was going to get through all of this. The view of Ted was incredibly depressing for him, yet he continued to display an upbeat and positive outlook on the business and on Ted. It was hard as he focused on the quiet hum of the oxygen tank that stood next to the couch.

He watched as Ted's gaunt, gray, emaciated appearance tried to function business as usual. The vile disease had wreaked havoc on Ted and in a matter of four months; his HIV status had escalated to full-blown AIDS. The purple lesions on his face and arms served as a constant reminder of the finality of the situation. Devin had learned more about the disease over the past several months than he ever needed to know because Ted had been back to the hospital twice since released. His condition was like a roller coaster, up and down. There were days when he could barely walk and others when his energy level was high.

Today was a down day. There was so much medication involved that if Ted had not been financially stable, he probably would have been dead already. Devin made regular trips to the pharmacy on his lunch break to pick up Ted's medication and then dropped them off after work. Each visit to the pharmacy was never less than one hundred dollars. The politics of obtaining the more advanced and effective medication was clear. If you had money, you could buy yourself some time with the best doctors and the best medication. But even with the aggressive treatments of Protease Inhibitors, Nucleoside Reverse Transcriptase Inhibitors and Non-Nucleoside Reverse Transcriptase Inhibitors in Ted's arsenal, it did not seem to be enough to prevent him from wasting away.

Devin had read that about half of people with HIV develop AIDS within ten years, but that the time between infection and onset varied greatly. Ted was not one of the fortunate cases that had experienced a long lag time between the two. Although, Devin was not sure that even Ted knew how long he had been infected with HIV. People were staying fit and well for many years since the symptoms varied from none to night sweats and recurrent infections.

Last week, Ted's CD4 count had dipped below 200, indicating that he was in the late stage of AIDS. Doctors were trying to bring the count back up, but admitted that they were not optimistic. Ted had been through having thrush, oral hairy leukoplakia, diarrhea and fatigue. His most recent symptoms were pneumocystic pneumonia, cytomegalovirus infection and Kaposi's Sarcoma; however, his significant weight loss was the scariest to Devin thus far.

Taylor had begun helping him pick up certain prescriptions that could be filled faster at other pharmacies in an attempt to relieve some pressure off of Devin. Certainly there were pharmacies that delivered, but her intentions were two-fold: to help

Devin and to portray herself in a less cynical and bitter light. No matter what she thought, Ted and Devin were friends. She could not change that. It was obvious that Ted was not doing well and the least she could do was support Devin during this time. For this Devin was thankful.

Initially he was concerned about Taylor reacquainting herself with her addiction, but they seemed to be in a good place right now.

"I think that'll do it," Ted said, signing the last document.

"Okay. You still sure about all of this?" Devin asked hesitantly.

Ted nodded his head and for the first time Devin fought hard to keep his own emotions at bay. This was not the Ted he knew. This Ted had confirmed he was ready to die with the last stroke of his pen. They both knew it.

"You realize this is a lot of money we're talking about. I just want to make sure you've thought this through," Devin said standing from the chair. "This is a lot of responsibility on my part, but I love you like a brother, which is the only reason I'm doing this," he added.

"I know," Ted replied weakly. "But time is of the essence."

"Why don't you go back to the hospital and let them treat you...keep you going, man."

"For what? For who?"

Devin turned and walked over to the picture window that seemed to look out onto the world. The day was bright, clear and crisp. Thanksgiving had come and gone. He had worked that day like any other, visited with Ted and then tried to spend some time with his family that evening. The enormity of all that was happening was almost too much to handle. Life was ebb and flow...bringing people into your life and taking others out.

"For you," Devin finally replied.

"This is where it'll happen. I'm not going back to the hospital to be poked, prodded and looked at like some pity case...another statistical anomaly that can't be figured out. This disease is crazy and it robs you of everything, but it won't take my ability to die with dignity."

Devin understood as much as was conceivably possible. He knew that as a man, dignity and pride often got you into trouble, but they were also the two things that made you a hero.

"I understand," Devin said taking the stack of documents from Ted. "I'll review these with the attorney and get copies back to you."

"Don't bother," Ted responded repositioning himself on the couch.

"So, what else do you need me to do?" Devin asked ignoring his friend's cynicism.

"I think we're all done," Ted replied wincing. His wincing turned into a snicker.

"What are you laughing about?" Devin asked totally astonished by this sudden mood change.

"I was just thinking about something really funny. You remember that time when we took that trip to Chicago a couple of years ago?"

"Yeah," Devin replied trying to follow where this was going.

"Me too. That was one of the best times I ever had, man. The game at Rigley Field, the clubs, the women. Man oh man! 'Ya know I've always taken the bull by the horns...just rushed right in, head first and you...well, you've always opted to take a moment and ponder things first. For so long man, I wished I could've had what you have. The wife, the kids, the routine, but it ain't in me. As bad as I wish it could've been, it's just not there. I have no misconceptions as to why I'm in this situation. My lifestyle dictated that it would be this or someone's husband put ting a bullet in my head," Ted laughed ruefully.

"Ted, no one deserves this. Maybe in your case you are a product of your lifestyle, but don't beat up on yourself. What about all the people who have received blood transfusions and the babies who are born with AIDS? There is just no rhyme or reason as to why anyone should be afflicted with this disease."

"Say what you will, but you've always told me everything happens for a reason and now I believe it."

"Look, you have to get past all of this negativity. The healthier your state of mind the better your outlook on life and on this disease."

"Yeah, I guess you're right," Ted agreed. He was silent for a while and all that could be heard was the hum from his breathing apparatus. "You know, I know Taylor never liked me."

"Hey man," Devin chuckled, "You know how it is."

"I wish I did. I wasn't sayin' it to put you on the spot; it's no secret. I guess I just want to say thanks for having my back, no matter what. You've always been there, like a brother. You and me always thought alike. We've always been about gettin' our money and I know that must've caused some tension between you and the wife."

"Don't even think about it. Much like you, the bed I've made, I gotta lay in it."

"You know what I miss most?"

"What's that?"

"Those Philly Cheese steak sandwiches from that little greasy spoon around the corner from the office. I barely have much of an appetite these days and when I do, I definitely can't eat anything like that," he said, sipping on a can of Ensure.

"Yeah," Devin agreed, "But that'll change as soon as you get your strength back."

"You are one painfully optimistic SOB," Ted joked. Both men laughed and for a moment it was like old times. The cur rent situation forgotten but for an instant. "Hey look man, you better get going, you've got a business to run…a legacy to leave for those boys."

"That's doing fine, just so you know."

"No surprise here. I never doubted there'd be success."

"Yeah, I guess so," Devin said as he stood and headed toward the door, "You hang in there and I'll check in with you tomorrow."

"I ain't going nowhere, I'll be right here," Ted responded, making a valiant effort to be upbeat.

"All right now." Devin closed the door behind him unsure of whether or not he would ever see his friend alive again.

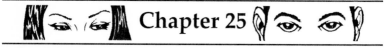 **Chapter 25**

Taylor sat on the couch, papers sprawled out before her, planning her 'To do' list for the day. She and Devin were hosting Christmas dinner at their house this year and there was much to do in preparation for twenty-two guests. The house was quiet and it was still early. She had been up for almost half an hour, curing the ham, seasoning the prime rib and soaking the greens.

She turned on the Christmas tree lights and placed last minutes gifts in the stockings before starting the hot cocoa. Any minute now, the boys would come racing down the stairs to demolish the neatly wrapped gifts. The seven-foot tree was positioned comfortably in the curve of the spiral staircase. Gifts spilled out from underneath the tree and into the walkway of the stairs and family room. The house was festive.

To her surprise, her boss had successfully negotiated awarding her the prestigious President's Award in addition to a hefty year-end bonus for her work on the successful rollout of the company's benefit package and a second company-wide rollout of the employee 401K and Stock Purchase Plan. That had been a huge undertaking that she scrambled to finish just two days ago. She smiled at the thought that her boss, Jim, never ceased to amaze her. He was crass at best and his tactics were really not suited for Corporate America, but rather some shipping dock, but he was definitely fair.

"I know it may seem like I give you a tougher time of things than I do the rest of the group, but it's because you do excellent work and I know you have the potential to go far," he had told her when giving her the awards. Taylor had been so shocked that she may have appeared ungrateful because she could not remember even saying thank you. In fact, she could not remember catching the elevator and walking back to her office. The two monetary gifts totaling sixty-three thousand dollars net was not a bad way to celebrate Christmas and ring in the New Year.

Taylor heard thumping overhead and knew that in seconds she would see Jr. and Chaz.

"I'll race you," she heard and then Chaz came barreling out of his bedroom with Jr. bringing up the rear.

"Hold on just a minute you two." Both boys stopped dead in their tracks with silly grins on their faces. "I want you to do two things...number one, I want you both to go and brush your teeth and number two...I want you to walk to the bathroom and walk back...no running, your father is still asleep, now go!"

The boys marched back to their bathroom and reappeared within minutes as they pretended to tiptoe by their parent's bedroom door. Just as they passed in front of the door, it swung open and out jumped Devin.

"Ahhhh, Merry Christmas," he growled like The Grinch.

The boys took off running down the stairs with Devin hot on their trail.

"Okay, okay you three. We don't want any accidents," Taylor scolded trying not to laugh.

Ignoring her, Devin, Devin Jr. and Chaz made their way to the tree and searched the gifts for their names. Devin Jr. carried away two large packages under each arm and took them to the sofa. Chaz never moved from in front of the tree. He had already gone through three presents before Jr. had begun opening one.

Devin feigned disappointment at not seeing anything for himself under the tree.

"Well, I guess Santa don't love me no more," he whined.

"We love you daddy," Chaz yelled. He then pulled a gift from under the tree that was wrapped in green construction paper.

"It's for you and mommy," Chaz said.

"Okay, we'll open it together," Devin said, tearing a strip of the paper of and handing it to Taylor who finished opening it.

"How beautiful, baby," Taylor said admiring the handmade Christmas ornament. "Isn't that nice?" she asked kissing Chaz on one of his chubby cheeks.

. "That is really nice, son" Devin agreed.

"Way cool!" Devin Jr. exclaimed admiring his new Sean John jacket. "Oh, I've got something for you too," Devin Jr. piped up. "It's in my room," he added.

"Could it be that you cleaned your room?" his dad joked.

"No, dad," Devin Jr. replied as if to say, you've got to be joking.

Devin Jr. ran upstairs to his room to get his gift.

"Well, my gift to you was too big to place under the tree so I put it in the den," Taylor said cheerfully.

"Like that?" Devin asked.

"Oh yes. Follow me."

Devin and Chaz followed behind her like school children being led out to the playground for recess.

"Wait for me," Devin Jr. yelled as be bounded down the stairs and fell in line.

Once inside the den, Taylor opened the closet and began pulling on a large box covered with a blanket.

"A little help here gentlemen," Taylor chided.

All three of them easily slid the box out into the middle of the floor. Taylor pulled off the blanket and listened to the collective sighs as their eyes focused on the pictures and writing on the box.

"Wow! Baby, this is just what I wanted," Devin exclaimed. He went to work opening the box to the forty-two inch plasma screen television.

"I'm glad you like it," Taylor said smiling.

"Oh yeah, this is sweet," Devin said. He stood and grabbed Taylor around the waist, hugging her and then planting a kiss on her lips. "Thank you baby."

"You're welcome."

"I'll get this set up shortly, but first, I have something for you too."

Devin trotted out of the den and into the living room where he extracted a small box out of one of the stockings that hung over the fireplace. He quickly returned and handed it to Taylor.

"For you," he said winking at the boys.

"Ooh," Taylor cooed. She carefully removed the wrapping paper and took a deep breath before opening the box. Slowly, she eased the box open and was rewarded with two brilliant diamond earrings glistening against their blue, velvet case.

"Oh Devin," Taylor managed. She placed her hand over her mouth hoping it would prevent her from crying.

"I take it you like them," Devin said smiling.

"They're gorgeous," Taylor said excitedly while still eyeing the precious stones.

"But they pale in comparison to you, baby. Merry Christmas!" Devin kissed his wife on the forehead.

"Ugh!" Chaz groaned.

They all laughed.

"Devin these are absolutely beautiful. Thank you."

"I'm glad you like them. I wish I could've gotten bigger ones, but they didn't have the clarity those babies have."

"You aren't doing too bad with these at all."

"I guess you're right. One carat each is nothing to sneeze at."

"No kidding. Thank you again," Taylor said, this time kissing her husband on the lips.

"Okay, okay. Can you guys open my gift now? We have way more stuff to open before everyone gets here," Devin Jr. said handing them a box that had been wrapped in newspaper.

"Okay," Taylor said, "We can open this one together. Now everyone help me out here." They all ripped into the present until they were down to the brown, cardboard box.

"Mom you finish opening it."

"All right." Taylor peeled back the piece of masking tape that held the box closed and pulled out the balled up newspaper that covered the gift. Sitting in the box was a ceramic, glazed sculpture of a house. It remarkably resembled their house in both shape and color.

"Wow DJ! This is the most beautiful artwork I've ever seen," Taylor exclaimed.

"That's really good. How long did it take you to finish it?" Devin asked.

"I've been working on it since the beginning of school. I didn't know if I was gonna finish, but I did. Our art teacher, Mr. Fessler, let me have extra time to finish glazing it last week."

"Well, this is going to be the centerpiece on our table this evening. Thank you baby," Taylor said kissing her son on his forehead.

"Mom, no!" Devin Jr. responded trying to get out of his mother's grasp. Devin and Chaz joined in to help hold Devin Jr. in place while Taylor repeatedly kissed him on his forehead and cheeks.

Guests began arriving at the Harris household for Christmas dinner at 2:00 p.m. The first to arrive were Devin's Uncle Lou and Aunt Francine followed by his mother, grandmother, sister and brother, five nieces and nephews and the infamous Uncle Graham.

On Taylor's side of the family, her mother Ruth and father Charles, three uncles, one aunt and two cousins, Camara and for Taylor, her most anticipated guest, Camara's boyfriend, Randolph Cellars. He was very much the opposite of what Camara's type used to be, he was white. He was handsome in a very masculine, non-descript sort of way...similar to Matt Damon. Most of all, he seemed very kind and genuinely infatuated with Camara, which led Taylor to easily understand why her friend was attracted to him.

Taylor had an agenda laid out for Christmas afternoon and evening. Half an hour after guests arrived they would have eggnog and board games. By 3:30 p.m. dinner would be served. Her cornbread dressing, smoked turkey, ham, potato salad, macaroni and cheese and mustard greens were enough to feed a small army. Everyone feasted to the point of bursting. By 4:30, those who drank, which were all the men, retreated to the family room to sip Cognac and chug beer by the fireplace while watching the football game on Devin's new television.

"Now I hope everyone in here has a designated driver," Taylor announced.

Everyone admitted that their wives, sons or daughters would be driving them home, except for Uncle Graham.

"Well, I'm stayin' the night so I plan on getting' lit." Uncle Graham announced. "If you need me, you can find me right here in front of this pretty television. Boy they sure have come a long way with these picture tubes these days. What y'all call this type TV...lava?"

"Plasma, Uncle Graham, plasma screen." Devin assisted.

"You're getting it confused with the lava lamps ya'll had back in the sixties, uncle," Trina said laughing.

Everyone chuckled, even Uncle Graham.

"You say you plan on getting' lit, huh?   I'd say you already there," Uncle Lou announced.

"I ain't too drunk to beat you in some pool," Uncle Graham responded.

Taylor left the room shaking her head. When she returned to the dining room, the women were still there gossiping, as women are known to do. Taylor couldn't resist.

"Okay, what are you all gossiping about? Let me in on it." They began cackling like hens.

"We were just talking about Camara's new beau," Aunt Francine spoke first.

"Yeah, the way he was pulling out her chair and hugging her during dinner, I thought he was gonna start feeding her and wiping her mouth too," Trina, Devin's sister added.

"Oooh girl, you a mess," Ruthie chimed in.

"See y'all like family and everything, but you definitely ain't right," Camara joked.

"Well clearly the man is in love or lust or something. What have you done to the brotha, Camara?" Taylor asked of her friend.

"Okay, I'm going in here with the men in a minute," Camara managed between fits of laughter.

The women sat for at least another hour with the elders sharing Christmas and Thanksgiving stories of their youth. Taylor always enjoyed the holidays. It seemed no matter how bad a year you had, Christmas made up for everything. Her year had been worse than usual, but today all that seemed like a distant memory. She looked around the table at her family and friends and thought about how blessed she truly was. How could she ever have let herself get to a point where she needed a drug to get her through with all the support she had sitting at this very table.

Only Devin and Camara knew about her problem and she planned to keep it that way.

"I'm ready for pie," she heard someone say, pulling her from her private thanksgiving.

"Where are the pies?" her mother asked.

"They're warming in the oven mom, but help yourself. Anyway, it's almost time for karaoke," Taylor announced.

"I'll go tell the guys," Camara offered.

The men, reluctantly pulled themselves from Uncle Graham's pool game and football.

"Okay, let's get this party started," Devin sang.

"I'm going to check on the kids and I'll be right back," Taylor said.

By the time she came back down the stairs, a full-fledged party had started. The sound bounced off the walls and reverberated throughout the house. Everyone was up on his or her feet dancing to *Got To Give It Up* by Marvin Gaye. Even Randolph seemed to be right at home and on beat.

Taylor joined in and danced through the crowd. His sister was instructing Devin on the finer points of the Harlem Shake. The seniors of the group had mastered the Electric Slide years ago and stuck to what they knew best. They danced every song from the Delphonics and the Temptations to Gerald Lavert and Ja Rule.

Devin, Taylor, Uncle Graham and Trina took turns being the disc jockey.

Uncle Graham sang a song by James Brown that entailed

more screaming that James himself could ever do. They all had a good laugh at his expense. You could always count on Uncle Graham for the laughs. When his song ended, it was Devin's turn to sing.

"This song I'm going to dedicate to my wife. A beautiful song for a beautiful woman."

Taylor knew Devin was a little buzzed, but she could tell his words were sincere and it touched her heart. With the first note of the song, Taylor knew what song she would be serenaded with, her favorite, *Differences* by Ginuwine. Devin turned up the volume and belted out a few tunes.

Taylor's eyes began to well up with tears. She knew she would not make it through the rest of the song. Maybe if he was a horrible singer like his Uncle Graham it would be different, but Devin could sing well and it was getting to her.

Taylor could hold back no more. The floodgates opened and tears flowed freely down her face. She felt these words before they were ever a song and now, here they were being put to a beautiful melody and sung by the man she loved. Devin took her by the hand as he crooned into the microphone. He danced with his wife in the middle of the floor with their families looking on.

When the song was over, Devin lifted Taylor's chin and wiped the tears away with the pads of his thumbs. He gave her a brief kiss on the lips.

"Merry Christmas," he grinned.

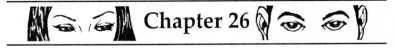 **Chapter 26**

Devin paced the small foyer until he began to see a pattern in the carpet. His palms were sweaty and his stomach churned as he struggled to keep the stinging sensation of bile from rising in his throat. He had been having these symptoms for the past two days but had not become accustomed to them. At some point, he knew he would lose the battle with his gag-reflex.

Taylor extended her hand, reaching for Devin to have a seat beside her on the bench. He took her hand to steady his own and with some resistance took a seat next to his wife.

"It'll be okay, baby," Taylor said, comforting her husband.

"I just can't believe this. I mean...it's not like I didn't know it was coming, but why'd it have to be so soon?" Devin pleaded.

"I don't know," Taylor replied, still holding Devin's hand in hers.

"I just wish there was something more I could do."

"Devin, you did everything you possibly could to make things run as smooth as possible. There was nothing, I repeat nothing more you could've done."

"I just can't believe Ted's not here anymore 'ya know. I

mean how is it that someone is here one day and not the next?"

"I know how hard this must be for you but you have to make sure things run smoothly. I contacted everyone in his Rolodex and Palm Pilot so there should be a huge turnout."

Devin was quiet and Taylor could tell he was a million miles away. She rubbed the side of his face and massaged his tense shoulders hoping he could pull it together before the guests began to arrive.

Ted Levingston had succumbed to his illness the day after Christmas. Devin had been so high in spirit on Christmas only to come crashing down to earth the very next day.

"Devin my grandmother always said that funerals should never be about death, but about celebrating a persons life. I'm sure you've heard it said that we should cry when babies are born and celebrate when people die. It's a hard concept to embrace, but if you think about it, it makes a whole lot of sense. Today should be about saying goodbye to a friend, which I know is hard, but he brought a lot of joy and happiness to your life and that alone is worth celebrating his life."

Devin stood without saying a word and turned towards his wife. He put his arms around her and hugged her fiercely, never wanting to let go, but knowing that he must. Ted had left him with a large responsibility to the tune of one point five million dollars and he had to find out how best to honor Ted's wishes as indicated in his will.

Taylor could hear guests beginning to arrive out front. She straightened Devin's tie and helped him compose himself. They walked into the church and sat in the front pew.

Within ten minutes the church was filled to capacity with the majority being women. Devin surveyed the crowd. There were some business associates, everyone from the office and at least one young lady he recognized as having had an intimate relationship with Ted.

Devin shook his head. He could only imagine what must be going through her head right now. Sadly, Ted had no family present. He never knew his father, his mother died in a car accident two years after he graduated college and he had no siblings, except for a half brother on his father's side whom he had never met. As far as the mourners attending the service were concerned, Ted had died of a rare and aggressive form of stomach cancer. Those who Ted had been intimate with, depending on their circumstances, might be drawing their own conclusions by now.

At promptly 11:00 a.m., Pastor Westfall started the service with a prayer and thanked the over four hundred guests in attendance. Taylor wondered if all the people there even knew Ted. She and Devin had been members at the church for over fifteen years and she could never remember seeing the church this full unless there was a wedding. She considered that some people just liked attending funerals for the sheer sake of attending. Ted had only been to their church once, but Devin felt there was some connection and semblance of home in having the service there. Being the only 'relative' Ted had, Devin felt it his responsibility to eulogize his friend...his brother. Pastor Westfall completed his opening remarks and turned the service over to Devin.

Devin took the podium and looked around the church to gauge the expressions on people's face. They ranged from shock and disbelief to pained and totally vexed. Devin removed his notes from the breast pocket of his suit jacket and spread them out onto the podium. He shifted his weight to his left foot and began:

"Uncompromising. Meticulous. Brilliant. Confident. These were all words that were attached to Ted Levingston throughout his life. But they were also words that described a man who changed the rules of obtaining the hottest music first for music lovers. Ted merged his artistic vision with music in a way that no other marketing and sales genius could. Ted's death came as a shock to me even though I knew he was ill. I can't imagine a day without him because we were like brothers," Devin said. He got choked up and had to take a moment to compose himself. He continued, "His legacy...our legacy...Mymelody.com will impact me personally as I continue to see our dream materialize. To be fair, Ted was frequently a tough and shrewd salesman. But his talent was so enormous, so all encompassing, so vast that somehow all the horror stories you may have heard seem justified. With Ted now gone, I wonder how different my life would've been if I had never known him. He was a giant of a man, unafraid to tackle the unknown and go after a unique vision. I can only hope that I will be able to singularly sustain the stature of his vision in the years to come. I'll miss you man," Devin concluded.

The crying commenced and Devin was relieved he had made it through the eulogy. He walked away from the podium and took his seat near Taylor, who covered his hand in hers.

Pastor Westfall preached a brief sermon that Taylor surmised must have required supreme discipline for him. Normally, it could take the pastor five minutes just to say hello. Maybe Devin had said all there was to say, the eulogy had been beautiful, she thought.

The sermon focused on telling people you loved them while they were living and living each day as if it were the last.

She felt a whirl of emotions. Guilt because Ted was dead and she never felt anything more than contempt for him when he was alive. While she never wished death on him or anyone, even now, she did not feel the remorse one feels when burying a friend either. Her sorrow originated more from seeing her husband in such an emotionally fragile state. Taylor wondered if she had become so desensitized over the years, that perhaps she was wrong for thinking the way she did. She had never consid ered herself an unforgiving person. She knew right from wrong and knew that the Bible instructed us to forgive seven times seventy. That resonated in her mind. She could no longer hate a person for being the way they were than she could for them being who they were. Taylor said a prayer for Ted and then for herself. No one deserved what happened to Ted and she hoped his final moments were peaceful.

The pastor closed out his sermon urging guests to pay their respects by saying goodbye to Ted. With the help of the ushers, guests assembled in an orderly fashion to view the body and say their final words. Taylor wondered why Ted did not request a closed-casket ceremony. The body that lay in the casket looked nothing like Ted. He was about fifty to sixty pounds lighter. His cheeks were sunken and his skin was two shades darker than his original coloring. Taylor could not bear to look at him and was glad she and Devin did not have to go up and say their farewells with the line of other people.

Devin sat numb next to his wife on the front pew in the church. Although the church was packed, he was considered the only 'family' member Ted had. Somehow that seemed even sadder to him than Ted's death. People walked by to view Ted's body. Devin could see some shaking their heads in disbelief, while others had to be helped past the casket. Condolences were offered to Devin and Taylor as the steady stream of people filed through the church and out the front doors.

Devin thought he noticed some disruption in the area nearest the front of the casket. People drew back, making it obvious who the culprit was. A tall brother with dreads was mouthing something that Devin could not make out. He was at a loss to determine who the man could have been talking to. He was horrified to see that he was screaming at Ted's corpse.

"Why did you do this to me?" the man yelled at the top of his lungs.

Devin and Taylor sat dumbfounded trying to figure out exactly what was happening. The man continued his ranting, "I'm glad you're dead!" the man shouted. He raised his fist as if he was about to strike the body and Devin bolted from his seat to stop him. The church security guard also came running down the aisle.

Devin was not fast enough and the man had struck Ted's body once already and was about to make contact again. Devin reached the man first and twisted his arm behind his back, forcing him to the ground as he hollered in pain. The security guard assisted in subduing the man and escorting him outside.

"Devin!" Taylor gasped.

"It's all right now," Pastor Westfall assured everyone.

"The devil is busy...even in the church. But we rebuke you today, devil. We rebuke you! Can I have a few of the choir members come up here."

Three women and one man from the church's choir went up on stage. One of the women took her seat at the organ. The choir began singing *Blessing in the Storm*.

Devin and the security guard escorted the man outside.

"Man, what's wrong with you acting like that at a funeral?" Devin asked, breathing heavily. "You need to get up outta here, now!" Devin demanded, not waiting for the man's response.

"Look," the man began.

"No, you look!" Devin said getting up in the man's face.

"Devin, don't do this," Taylor pleaded from the steps of the church. The security guard managed to get in between Devin and the man.

"I don't know what the problem was between you and Ted, but you won't settle it here today," Devin continued.

"You're right, man," the man said backing away with a pained expression on his face. Devin noticed that the man looked as if he had not slept in weeks. "I won't settle it here today or ever. 'Ya see my life is over because of your boy," the man spat.

"Look, if you're trying to get money or something--"

"Money?" the man laughed. His laugh was hollow and devoid of humor.

"You don't get it do you?" he asked. "Your boy was gay, but you might know that better than me."

The words sent Devin reeling. Before he knew it, he had gone after the man with everything he had. He threw a punch that whistled through the air, just missing the side of his head and immediately followed with another. The security guard made a futile attempt to stop Devin before moving out of the way.

Devin was in a blind rage that went deeper than the insult this complete stranger had made. He was enraged because he had lost a friend and no one could say anything to make him feel better. This guy was only making matters worse, which made him the perfect object of Devin's rage.

Devin managed to grab hold of the man's jacket and pull him back. He raised his fist to administer a blow that was certain to make contact.

"Devin, No!" Taylor screamed, running toward her husband. The security guard held her at bay. A small crowd of onlookers had convened on the church steps. Devin released the man, repulsed by the startling news and his own actions. A church was supposed to be a sanctuary from evil.

"Just go man," Devin motioned towards the man who was now on the verge of tears.

Taylor rushed to Devin's side, " Let's just go to the burial site," she offered.

They climbed in the back of the waiting limousine. As the driver pulled away from the curb, Devin pondered what the man had said. *Who was he?* he thought and what skeletons did Ted have in his closet that Devin did not know about. He had been through enough surprises to last him a lifetime. Right now, he just wanted to say goodbye to his friend.

 **EPILOGUE**

Six months later...

Taylor sat across the table from Diane surprised at her resolve. The last time she saw Diane in her office was over a year ago and Diane was a weeping mess, whining about her secretary not doing her job. She was now explaining to Taylor that the whole period with her former assistant, Rosalind Perez was during a dark stage in her life.

Taylor knew the truth. The corporate grapevine worked no different from the one in the hood. Everyone knew Diane and her husband had reconciled. Diane had all but climbed to the top of the building and yelled it for all to hear. Everyday of her life had been a dark stage prior to her reconciliation with her husband. Taylor could identify with Diane's new outlook on life and was genuinely happy for her.

She too had a dark period in life, yet she was sure they had handled their issues differently. However, the end results were the same...their marriages were still in tact.

"So, I just decided life is too short. I don't want to be tied down to a nine to five all day. Stan and I are going to live in Paris for three months and then Australia."

"That's terrific!"

"Yeah, we think so," Diane joked.

"Well, you know how the saying goes, everybody ain't able."

"Oh, I don't buy into that. You and I both make good money as well as our husbands, but I don't think anyone would classify us as rich. For me, it's about quality of life. Would I rather sit around and talk about all the things I plan to do once I retire? Or do them now while I'm still young enough to enjoy the adventure. I can get another job. Sure, it may or may not pay what I'm making here, but my skills are transferable."

"Diane, I really admire your attitude. I say go for it!"

"I am."

"So when's your last day?"

"The end of July."

"A mere three weeks."

"You bet! That's why I wanted to get all my paperwork in order. But I also wanted to say thanks for being a friend. You got me through some pretty rough times and I appreciate it. All the stuff that had nothing to do with work...you listened," Diane said hugging Taylor. "I think you should have your boss's job."

"I think so too, but we don't need to let him know that."

"Diane I'm just glad you're happy," Taylor responded as she returned the favor. "Just do me a favor?"

"What's that?" Diane asked pulling away and now holding Taylor's hands.

"Bring me something back from the Land Down Under!"

Devin concluded his meeting with the board. He had been dreading it for the past two weeks, but everything had gone well and the projected forecast for Mymelody.com looked good.

The nine Caucasian men, two Caucasian women, two African-American men and one African-American women seemed to finally be convinced that the company had sustainability even in Ted's absence and that he had in fact died of stomach cancer. After the scene at the funeral home, Devin was even more committed to ensuring his friend's dignity and reputation remain in good standing.

Devin wondered about the mysterious man who showed up ranting and raving. The things he said haunted Devin, but they were insinuations that Devin was not prepared to entertain. Devin's biggest concern had been revealing Ted's death to the press, particularly The Street. But surprisingly, it had made the hits to their site and their stock soar.

In fact, Devin hired two new Development Directors and a Marketing Vice President to help add structure and focus to their new initiative; the ability to not only download music, but also the music videos, if available. The board was excited about the new features Mymelody.com would soon be offering its customers. Currently, there was nothing like it. Devin and Ted had been working on the concept for the past year. Devin smiled, reflecting on his friend. He would be celebrating now if he were here. Things were definitely not the same in the office without Ted, but Devin was committed not only to keeping their legacy going, but making it flourish.

He logged out of his computer and began straightening the stacks of papers on his desk. He headed out of his office and toward the door. Everyone had left except for his new Marketing Vice President, Matt Paulson.

Matt's complete attention was focused on the document displayed on his computer screen.

"Save some for tomorrow," Devin joked. "There are still four days left in this week."

Matt merely gave him a weary-eyed smiled.

"Gotta love a newbie," Devin said more to himself than to Matt.

He headed out the door and almost ran into a beautiful woman with skin the color of honey. She had shoulder-length hair and a tall, shapely frame. Her voice was soft, almost melodic.

"Are you Devin Harris?" she asked.

"Yes," he replied.

"We need to talk."

"What? Ted has a son?" Taylor asked in disbelief.

"Yeah, I couldn't believe it either," Devin agreed.

"Who is this mysterious woman?"

"Her name is Tracey Wells and she's someone Ted dated."

"Oh my goodness! Did they date up until he learned he was sick?"

"Off and on, but unfortunately, I think so."

"Is she?..."

"I don't know."

"What about the child?"

"I don't know. We didn't get into all that."

"Well, how do you know it's really Ted's?"

"She showed me the birth certificate and Ted told me he thought he had a son, but Tracey didn't want anything to do with him because he wasn't ready to get married."

"But he signed the birth certificate?"

"I suppose he did."

"Seems like there was a lot going on in Ted's life."

"Yeah, I think that would be putting it mildly."

"Sounds like a real mess."

"That's true, but I think he really cared about her. In fact, she was probably the only one. It's bizarre how things work out. I mean you would think he would have kids everywhere, but he was methodical in the way he did things. I'd be willing to bet he way okay with Tracey getting pregnant. But, Ted just did not have it in him to settle down," Devin said reflectively.

"Hmmm. So what exactly did she say? What does she want?"

"Well, she wanted me to know that she and Ted have a son. She said Devin talked about me to her all the time. She knew we were business partners and knew that Ted trusted me."

"So she was counting on exactly what Ted did...make preparations for his son?"

"Basically, yes."

"How old is the boy? And what's his name?"

"Little Ted Maurice Levingston is ten months old and named after his father. He's a cute boy. She showed me pictures."

"Well, what are you going to do?"

"I'm going to honor the stipulations of Ted's will and provide for his son. As his trustee, that's what I'm obligated to do. Ted had very specific plans for the allocation of his assets. That really helps me a lot. Long-term, I'll be there for whatever the boy needs"

"You know, I think Ted was lucky to have you as a friend," Taylor said, kissing Devin gently on his cheek.

"I don't look at it like that. I know he would've done the same for me. Ted really was a good person. In the end, he was just a man who had a rather warped outlook on life and relationships, but it didn't make him a bad person. He designated a quarter million dollars to AIDS research."

"That's wonderful. I just know they'll have a cure some day. They just have to."

"Yeah, I'm sure they will. I just wish it could've been

discovered in time to save my friend."

The last Saturday of June was one of the most beautiful days of the year. The weather was warm, without being burdensome and the smell of summer clung to the air. Birds and butterflies floated through the air and seemed to disappear into the heavens. The same church where Taylor and Devin attended a funeral service some months ago now took on a bright and festive tone with its champagne and cream-colored accents.

The church was full but for a happy occasion.

Camara made a beautiful bride. Her dress, much like their wedding was simple, yet elegant. Taylor was happy for her friend and had been moved to tears by her wedding vows.

"I, Camara choose you, Randolph, as my best friend for life. Our love may be like the ebb and tide of the ocean, but it will always flow. When you need someone to encourage you, I want it to be me. When you need a helping hand, I want it to be mine. When you long for someone to smile at, turn to me. When you have something to share, share it with me.

From this moment, I pledge to honor, encourage, and support you through our walk together. When our way becomes difficult, I promise to stand by you and uplift you, so that through our union we can accomplish more than we could alone. I promise to work at our love and always make you a priority in my life. With every beat of my heart, I will love you. This is my solemn vow.

I vow to be patient with you and the circumstances in our lives. I vow to be kind to all people we come across. I vow not to be boastful of our love or about our accomplishments. I promise to be proud of you, but not proud in love for though I will strive for perfection, I know I can never reach it. I promise not to be quick to anger, but to think before I speak and act. I vow not to keep a record of wrongs, but to always keep the happy memories alive. Through God, our love will never fail."

Taylor could tell that Camara had found true love. She had heard it said that love meant never having to say you were sorry. That could be deciphered two different ways. Did it mean that no matter how much pain you caused your spouse you never had to apologize because the mere fact that you were married meant you were loved? Or, did it mean that that you never committed an act against your spouse that put you in a position to have to apologize in the first place?

Love meant different things to different people. So much had happened over the past two years that changed her outlook on life. To her, loving those around you meant loving yourself enough to do everything possible to be there and in a healthy state of mind for them. Love also meant supporting family and friends and keeping the lines of communication open so that there could be no room for speculation or conjecture. But most important, love meant that you did not have to blame yourself for the mistakes others made. Deep down inside, she had blamed herself for Devin's actions, which was why she looked for solace and a way out. She could not rationalize that any more than she could the many reasons women often blamed themselves when things went wrong in their relationships. However, experience had been a good teacher. She was strong now and did not need the aid of pills to help her escape her problems. She faced them head on. Nothing miraculous had happened in her life other than some very defining moments that reminded her of how short life could be. God was still there. He always had been…waiting for her to find her way. Simply put, there were things she had accepted before that would no longer be tolerated. It was a primal defense developed purely out of the need of self-preservation.

175

She and Devin sat amongst the other guests as the pastor announced Mr. and Mrs. Randolph Cellars. Taylor had been holding Devin's hand. He squeezed her hand a little tighter when the pastor announced the new couple. She looked at her husband's handsome profile and at their two sons whose attention was focused where hers should have been, on the recessional of Camara and Randolph.

Pain had been replaced by peace, understanding and forgiveness not only of Devin, but of herself.

Taylor raised she and Devin's intertwined hands to her lips and kissed the back of her husband's hand. It was about the simple things for her: sitting next to her husband, just enjoying the moment, this was what love meant to her.

ANNA DENNIS
has been writing for six years.
She has written several children's short stories and has
had commentary published in Essence Magazine.
Familiar with the literary industry, she was a presenter
at the1997 Sister Circle Book Club Awards in San Francisco
and formerly co-owned Black Spring Books in
Vallejo, California.
She is co-founder of The Bay Area Book Writer's Guild
whose mission is to inspire and educate aspiring writers
through networking events.
She lives in California with her husband and daughter.
This is her second novel.